D1554634

The Killer

The Killer

STEVEN HAVILL

DOUBLEDAY & COMPANY, INC.

GARDEN CITY, NEW YORK

1981

All of the characters in this book are fictitious, and any resemblance to actual persons, living or dead, is purely coincidental.

First Edition

ISBN: 0-385-17287-7
Library of Congress Catalog Card Number 80-1987
Copyright © 1981 by Steven Havill
All Rights Reserved
Printed in the United States of America

for Kathleen

The Killer

CHAPTER 1

Jody Burton started it all. There's no doubt in my mind, or in the minds of anyone else who remembers that fall of 1885 in the tiny village of Ludlum, Wyoming Territory.

A question of buckets was all it was, at the beginning. Jody used an old, serviceable wooden bucket that was worn and slick, a bucket that the Burtons had used for years. And in that bucket, she mixed the first innocent ingredients of a two-month nightmare. In the weeks that followed, other people would leave their marks to be recalled more vividly, but I guess it's fair to say Jody started it all.

The water supply for the Burton household was first a spring that burbled out of the hillside fifty yards behind the roughhewn clapboard cabin. Paul Burton had said for several years that he intended to run a pipe from that spring right into the cabin. He had never purchased the pipe, but he had built a kind of cistern inside, next to the cookstove. The water continued to be brought to the cabin by the bucketful, poured into the cistern for household chores.

During that crackling dry summer of 1885, the spring continued to flow undiminished. Paul was proud of that and said several times that he was going to order fifty yards of pipe through Woodstock's Feed and Supply in Ludlum, a mile south of his ranch. The village of Ludlum didn't share the good fortune of his spring. In fact, several dozen families not lucky enough to have wells of their own depended on Ghost Creek, a mountain ribbon that raced past the Burton ranch and then wandered down the valley through the east edge of the village, to join finally just south of Ludlum with the Little Muddy River.

When even Ghost Creek threatened to dry to nothing more than a gravel path, Burton's spring still flowed.

The dry summer came to an end violently, a little after three in the morning on a late August Tuesday, just a few hours before Jody Burton picked up the wrong bucket.

Too many previous empty threats had conditioned folks in the area to ignore thunder. But this rumbling was no idle product of heat lightning. Although the people ignored it, the livestock knew better.

Burton's two geldings and his mare and colt all smelled the rain when it was still miles away and went dizzy. That wonderful smell grew to a cascading torrent of aroma spilling down the valley, and the four horses went to meet the weather—right through the flimsy fence Paul Burton had always insisted was strong enough. Burton, half asleep, heard the colt nicker uncertainly as the livestock trotted past the cabin, and it took him several seconds to realize that the animals were loose. Ten minutes later, the first rain of a two-hour cloudburst opened up over the valley.

By six in the morning, the storm diminished to a steady, hard drizzle and the men—Burton, Randy Kane from just up creek, and Cyril Garcia from the shack a thousand yards below Burton's ranch—tried to drive the wet chill from their bones. The livestock was back, steaming in the corral, but the three men were so wet they had started to prune. Jody made coffee and heavy flapjacks with the last of the milk and even served up some pie. By the time the three men went out again, this time to save Garcia's shack from sliding over the crumbling creek bank, the Burton home was a mess of puddles from the slickers and mud from the boots. Jody knew right then that it was going to be a long day.

There were pots and pans to wash, dirty clothes waiting—and an empty cistern. Jody put on a slicker and picked up the heavy wooden bucket by the door, hesitating only a second before trudging off through the rain and the slop to the spring. The small reservoir where the spring issued from the rocks was a rich muddy brown, and Jody brought back to the cistern five bucketfuls that were more mountain mud than spring water. The roily mixture would settle out, she knew, and she started on a sixth trip. The cow interrupted her progress.

Ignored during the morning's excitement, the cow was congested and impatient for relief. Jody remembered that the animal had not been milked, and she changed course for the small pole barn that stood a few yards away, just behind the privy. As Jody entered the barn, the cow looked up dimly from the dry straw, as if wondering what she had missed during her night-long manufacture of milk.

Jody hooked the plank stool over with her foot and put the bucket down in the straw. She stopped short and cussed an unladylike oath. Paul had ordered a shiny metal milk pail from an outfit in Chicago just that summer. It had been two dollars cheaper than Woodstock's best. Jody had thoroughly enjoyed the musical sound of the milk squirting onto the new metal, and even the cow had seemed vaguely pleased. But now Jody had the old wooden bucket and the new milk pail was in the cabin, what seemed miles away through the rain. She cursed her forgetfulness again, and looked closely at the wooden bucket. She shrugged. It looked clean enough, with just scant traces of water left in the bottom from the spring. She positioned the bucket under the animal and went to work. The cow chewed quietly and didn't seem to notice the difference. And so the fresh, warm milk and the water from the storm-filled spring came to mix.

That week that broke the drought was to pass quickly enough for Dr. John Farraday. Despite the mud in the streets, he enjoyed the rain, even when it lasted beyond its initial welcome. Doc Farraday enjoyed everything, especially the complications of human nature. His light brown eyes always looked at people as if they were part of some grand experiment the doctor was conducting. The rain and the mud only added spice.

Tuesday afternoon, when the rain still occasionally pounded following its early morning onslaught, Elizabeth DelRey stepped out of the El Grande Hotel to see a miniature river running down the middle of the street. Her ten-dollar Kansas City slippers had slipped on the wet pine planks of the boardwalk, most ungracefully. She hadn't gotten too muddy, but her right ankle was the size of a watermelon, and Doc Farraday had taken considerable time caressing the sprain and comparing it with the shapely left ankle, and caressing that too. Betsy was too white with pain to notice that the healthy ankle was receiving equal attention.

Doc was interrupted by Harv Wilcox, who didn't knock. Harv was missing his right thumb, and his lack of courtesy was understandable. He did sit still, though, while Farraday sewed up the messy stump. Betsy DelRey, her foot deep in a pan of hot water and epsom salts, turned so she couldn't see the procedure. But she could hear Harv's matter-of-fact voice describing how the rope had gotten kinked and then how he had slipped just as the pony had lunged back.

"Damn fool kind of day to be working with horses anyway," Farraday growled unsympathetically, and glanced over at Betsy. She was sitting with her eyes closed, one hand over her mouth.

Things were pretty much that normal throughout the week, until Sunday, when the doctor spent the whole day trying to keep J. J. Baker alive. Baker didn't want to be alive, which was how he happened to fall under Farraday's care in the first place. Evidently the five days of overcast had brought on Baker's glooms more than usual, and the old man had tried the direct approach. He'd held the Winchester a little askew, though. The slug had blown out just about everything but Baker's brain, and Farraday took the treatment of the gored-up head as a kind of personal challenge. He succeeded for seven hours, but after that Baker got where he wanted to go after all.

Farraday told me about it later, in some detail, when I went to talk to him about Baker for the newspaper files.

"Bad weather," Farraday said after I got what I needed on Baker. "Bad weather, this. One, two days is fine, but this is getting on people's nerves." Farraday straightened up. "Could have predicted about old Baker. Weather does that to a man that's down. Human body is resistant to a lot of things, but weather's not one of 'em. You watch, Patrick, old friend. By the end of this month, half the population of Ludlum will be down with the grippe. Just from the weather."

Looking back, I wish Farraday had been right. His prediction would have been far more welcome than what did happen. But we had little time to discuss it. I was busy, he was busy. And one day later, John Farraday, M.D., was dead.

The next Monday morning, when I last saw Farraday alive, was a relief from the week past. Although a wet haze was still in the air, the sun was out and so hot that most of the building roofs were steaming by mid-morning. My Monday routine involved nothing more complicated and erudite than a pair of scissors and my twice-a-week's mail via stage and the Union Pacific Railroad. I clipped and snipped, and before noon most of my front page had been fleshed out.

Even with that help, though, a small weekly newspaper sometimes can be hard to fill—especially when the past week had brought no news but the weather and one suicide. And so I was snipping a little more than usual when Farraday came through the front door.

"Morning, Doc," I called, carefully trimming around the fifth installment of *Jane Hexley's Romance*, which I was running in the Ludlum *Herald* with the unknowing compliments of the Chicago *World Telegraph*. I glanced up and smiled, and then stopped smiling when I saw Farraday's pale face. He looked worried, and that was unusual for Farraday, who took about everything in stride.

"Put away your journalistic scalpel and let me buy you a cup of coffee," Farraday said, but the good humor seemed forced, and he looked over at my typesetter, Jimmy Flower, who wasn't paying any attention—either to Farraday or to the work he was supposed to be doing. Leaning over my desk, Farraday spoke in almost a whisper: "Let's go, I need to talk to you."

I could see now that he was sweating more than usual, and plainly upset. "Sure, Doc," I said, and put the scissors down. "Jimmy, when you get done there, if you ever do, here's some more." I turned to the impatient doctor. "He's in love, Doc," I said, but Farraday didn't answer. I followed him out the door.

Farraday didn't say a word until we had seated ourselves in the back corner of the El Grande, and until Chase had brought over the coffee and left again.

"Doc, you look sick," I said, laughing.

Farraday frowned and wiped his forehead. "Patrick, I need your advice." Seeing my eyebrows go up, he grinned thinly. "I know, I'm the doctor," he said. "I'm not sick, but I need your help. I've just been upriver, and I think this town's going to have . . ." He was interrupted as the front

door of the El Grande crashed open and Milt Haley burst in
at full charge. Marshal Haley was banty rooster-sized, but
by God, he had a voice.

"Doc! We needja. Young Benny Pepper's had a huntin'
accident with his brother, for Christ's sake." Farraday was
already on his feet.

"Where is he?"

Haley was at the door, holding it for the doc. "Out at the
ranch, I guess. Billy come into town, and he says they're
scared to move him. You get your stuff and I'll fetch us
horses."

"My buckboard's still rigged," Farraday said, and without
so much as a backward glance, he was out the door and jog-
ging across and down the street toward his office.

What happened next was one of those accidents that is
hard for a small town to accept. As it was, Benny Pepper
didn't need Doc Farraday. His brother Billy had swung his
pop's old double Remington on some quail without paying
attention, and the charge had made Billy an only child.
Benny had been dead for five minutes when Doc ran out of
the El Grande for his medical bag.

It was two miles down the river road to the Pepper ranch,
and Marshal Haley didn't spare the team. A thousand yards
before the cut-off to the Peppers', the road narrows some,
right along the edge of the Little Muddy River. A massive
grove of cottonwoods makes the corner a blind one, and the
freight wagon driver, half drunk as he was and running for
time on a bet, never saw the light buckboard. Haley just had
time to lunge backward on the reins as the charging team of
eight hurtled around the corner and forced him and Doc
and the light buckboard off the road. The rain-weakened
riverbank crumbled, and the buckboard flipped over and
into the river, upside down. Marshal Haley came up gasp-

ing, but Doc Farraday never did. He was found later, caught under the wagon, his neck broken.

The driver of the empty freighter, whipping his horses back from the railhead to the Cavenaugh sawmill just north of Ludlum, never stopped.

CHAPTER 2

Big news always comes close to presstime in the newspaper business, and Doc's death was no exception. I frantically searched my mental files for everything I knew about John M. Farraday, M.D., and came up with only enough copy to displace about two good paragraphs of *Jane Hexley's Romance*. For a leading citizen of the town, that wasn't much—or enough.

With the import of the moment, I made the only decision open to me—or at least the only palatable decision. Since more time was needed to do justice to Farraday, what with a proper eulogy and all, presstime would have to be set back. That's easy to do when you own the paper and sure a whole lot easier than running about like a frantic cub reporter facing his first deadline. But my problems were small compared to the problems faced by the town as a whole.

Ludlum is isolated. The village is nearly forty miles from Fort Bridger, and thirty miles from the railhead, where the Union Pacific passes on its westerly route from Laramie to Evanston and finally Ogden, passing north of Fort Bridger. A stage line north–south links Denver to Fort Bridger, intersecting the railhead north of the Fort, and then winding up the valley to Ludlum and Kemmerer. Ludlum's twelve hundred souls had gathered as a village not a long stone's throw from the Little Muddy River, a sorry excuse for a watercourse whose only fame is being a tributary of the Gunnison. Unlike the founders of many of the mining settlements, the folks who settled Ludlum had come to the valley for no single reason. Ranching was good, except for the brutal weather during the winter and periodic dry terms that parched the prairie in the summer. The timber on nearby hills was still tall and endless, and at least three men were becoming rich as lumbermen. Winter played havoc with that business too, but the major headache was transportation. The heavy freight wagons hauled the logs and later the lumber to the railhead, but Will Cavenaugh, who was sixty-four years old and still stronger than most of the massive-girthed firs he cut, echoed the feelings of the other lumbermen as he constantly cussed the Little Muddy for not carrying enough water to float a log boom. One log crosswise in the Little Muddy at Ludlum was like catching a chicken bone in your throat—it stopped up the whole works.

A few men stuck to the real mountain profession of prospecting—but it was obvious that not much panned out. In the spring of 1879, Howie Nussbaum found one nugget as big as a thimble. He got so excited that he died of heart failure that evening in the El Grande, his mouth still full of free beer. Apparently it was an orphan nugget, because the rest of its relatives never turned up. Howie never knew that he excited himself to death over a hundred bucks.

Any town needs a few choice citizens. I'd like to include myself among them, of course. I had retired after years of living in the stench of Chicago and its stockyards, and working for one of its giant newspapers. I came to Ludlum for the solitude, for the eye appeal, for a change.

But Dr. Farraday was more to the town than that. Few were as much needed, and as sorely missed, as John M. Farraday. He had come to Fort Bridger as a bachelor army surgeon, served out the last two years of his hitch, and stayed in the area as a civilian, enjoying the hunting and fishing and people for three short years. When he was killed, he was forty-eight years old and had saved three times that many lives in Ludlum.

With a sigh, I put my pencil down. I'm not the type to stay morose for too long, and working on Farraday's story was bringing on a real case of the melancholies. I got up, made sure Jim was still mooning over the fonts (Flower was slow, but he didn't give me any yap. I'd had enough of cranky typesetters on the *World Telegraph*. I liberally stole their newspaper's copy as a kind of distant revenge), and stepped out into the street. The mud was beginning to crust at the crest of each sloppy wave turned up by the wagon and horse traffic, and I stepped gingerly. I wanted to see Milt Haley, figuring he'd be in his office a few doors down. With the bad wrench his knee had taken during the accident that killed Farraday, it wasn't likely that he was going anywhere for a few days.

I was right. I opened the raw oak door to the village marshal's office and found Haley sitting back, both legs up on his desk, a large wad of soft quilt under his left knee and a large glass of amber medicine in his left hand.

Many people hate Milt Haley's guts the moment they meet him. I hadn't thought much of him myself until I'd known him for two years. Small, thin, and loud, he tends to give people the impression that everything is fine as long as everyone agrees with him. That may be partly true, but thanks to Haley, Ludlum is a quiet place to live.

"How's the knee?" I asked by way of greeting.

Haley ducked his chin and belched. He waved the glass at me. "I'm soakin' it. Want some?"

I shook my head, and Haley belched again.

"Will Cavenaugh trussed up that no-good that drove us off the road and delivered him up this mornin'. Seems he was even boastin' about runnin' someone offin the road." He swung his legs down and winced. "Really galls me, though, Patrick, that the bastard never even stopped. I mean, hell, I've run my share of horses on a bet myself." He took another long drink of the whiskey and stared at the floor. "Damn," he finally said, as if summing up the whole affair, and looked at me reproachfully, like maybe I had the answer.

"What are you going to do with him now?" I asked, half sorry that I had missed the confrontation between Haley and the freight driver when Cavenaugh brought the man back to town.

"He's goin'," Haley said simply. "Cavenaugh up and fired him, and I'm havin' Bud Brown escort him down to Bridger on the stage today. Circuit judge's passin' by the Fort this week, and he can decide what to do with him. I drew up a real formal disposition listin' everything I could think of that might hang the bastard. Probably won't nothin' come of it, though."

I nodded. "Old Doc wanted to talk to me earlier yesterday, just before you came to fetch him. Sure seemed upset, especially for him. He say anything on the way out to Peppers' before the accident?"

"Nobody said a goddamn thing, the way I was drivin'. Lot of good it did. We coulda walked and it wouldn'ta made no difference to young Pepper. Sure woulda to Doc, though." Haley was obviously beginning to feel the mellowing effects of the liquor, and I could see he was blaming himself pretty heavily . . . but there was sure no good news to cheer him up that I could see.

"Well, then, one thing I do know is that winter's just three months or less away, and this town's going to need another doctor," I said. "How do you figure we go about getting ourselves one?"

Haley snickered unkindly. "You could advertise for one in your paper."

"Yep," I said, flashing my most winning smile, "at last count, there's three people outside of this town who read the *Herald*, and that's counting my own mother in Boston."

"You sure she reads it?" Haley cracked, and then suddenly he was serious again. "Well, hell, I don't know what we're goin' to do. The whole town's upset. I mean, much as we all thought highly of ole Doc, it's the man's medicine that everyone misses right now." He pointed at his knee. "And I ain't no exception." He took another swallow of whiskey and looked melancholy. "I liked the old army fart, Patrick."

"So did I, but that's past," I said. "Maybe we ought to wire Fort Bridger and ask Colonel Carlson if he can send up one of Dr. Patterson's assistants for a while. That's better than nothing." But Haley killed the idea quickly.

"Patterson's assistants, bull. He's got himself just one now. I already checked last night. Had Bud run a message to the telegraph in case there was someone at the Fort who coulda rode up here today. But Patterson ain't about to cut his staff any more, active as that Fort is. In fact, the colonel gave me a flat no. As far as the army doc from Bridger goes, we're on the other side of the territory." Haley grimaced and shifted his leg. "Think of somethin' else."

He pulled out his watch, then leaned forward to look at the old wall clock he kept just to one side of the window. Haley stood up stiffly and stretched, repocketing the watch.

"About stage time," he said, and limped carefully to the door.

The door opened just as he reached for the latch, and Bud Brown stepped in. He nodded at me and turned to point at his bedroll on the boardwalk behind him.

"I'm all set, Milt," he said.

Haley turned to let Bud step by into the room. "Keep a keen eye on that son-of-a-bitch, Bud," he said. "I don't sus-

pect he'll try nothin', particularly after that wallop old Cavenaugh gave him. Army'll meet you at the Bridger stage
stop and keep him set until the judge gets to 'em." We could
hear the rattle of the stage, and Haley waved at the cell
door in the rear of the building. "Bud, you might as well get
him on out of there. He's still shackled and all, but if he
gives you any trouble, why, you just blow his head off,
okay?" Bud smiled and vanished into the back room that
was barred off into two cells.

Haley, with his hand on the doorjamb, limped carefully
out into the sunlight. "I'm goin' out on the porch and set,"
he said. "Make my duly appointed show as law and order
for any strangers that might be comin'." He grinned despite
the pain as he lurched to an ancient cane chair with a half-
rotted seat that leaned against the wall just outside the door.
"Don't tell 'em about my knee," he said, settling into the
chair. "If someone up and asks you why the marshal don't
ever get out of his chair, you just tell 'em I died two weeks
ago and it's too wet for buryin'."

Haley needn't have worried, though. The stage rolled
through the mud into Ludlum, halting just long enough to
change teams and drivers, pick up Bud Brown and his
bruised and contrite passenger, and leave behind a small
bag of mail from Kemmerer. Thirty minutes later, it was
gone, leaving the town quiet. Those two days were about
the last peaceful days Ludlum was to have.

Our lives were changed two days later, on Thursday,
when the stage reversed its route and headed back up the
valley.

When the Thursday stage clattered into town, Haley was
back on the porch, knee propped up on the banister, waiting
to see if Bud had made the trip all right. I always try to
meet the stage, I guess out of professional interest and no-
siness most of the time. You never know what news is going

to step down. So I sat on the rail next to Haley, and saw with satisfaction that the stage carried passengers other than Bud Brown, who lighted first, came over, and briefly recounted his trip to Haley, then took off up the street toward his home to "see the little woman." We turned our attention to the other arrivals.

One of the passengers I knew, the other was a stranger. Florence Buchanan had been to Laramie for nearly a month visiting an ailing sister, and she audibly creaked as she stepped down. My family would have to be mighty ailing to get me to make that trip if I was pushing eighty like Florence. The stranger waited until Florence was well clear of the step before he ventured out. Thin and pale, he didn't stand more than five feet tall, and the dark suit he was wearing wasn't the best of fits. The hawk-sharp face turned by us like we didn't exist, and the man looked up the street, obviously searching for someone. The stage driver said something we didn't hear, and the stranger turned back to the coach, reaching up to catch a solid valise that the driver handed him from among the rear luggage. Nodding politely to Mrs. Buchanan, who beamed happily back, the small stranger set off up the street.

"Queer lookin' dude," Haley said, none too softly. Florence Buchanan, waddling from the stage, obviously overheard him, and steered her way over to where I stood and Haley sat. I tipped my hat and Haley leaned forward in his seat.

"Welcome back, Miz Buchanan," he said gallantly. "Pardon me if I don't stand up, but I busted my knee." He jerked his head after the retreating stranger. "Who's your partner?"

Florence bridled. "That gentleman is neither queer looking *or* a dude," she snapped. "I had a most pleasant trip, and I'm here to say that he eased my aching joints considerable." She paused for dramatic emphasis, and shouldn't have.

"I didn't know you drank," Haley interjected, with the typically superb timing that always made me wince.

Florence Buchanan glared daggers at the marshal. At that point, no one ever would have guessed that she regularly sent baked goodies to his office as a constant reminder that she appreciated being safe in her own bed.

"You are an oaf," she said crisply. "That 'queer looking dude,' as you so very rudely call him, is our own Dr. John Farraday's cousin from Denver, Mitchell Whitman." She raised her nose several notches in the air. "He is not only a fine gentleman but a fine physician as well." She mistook Haley's look of astonishment as one of proper contrition. "We shall all make him welcome," she concluded, and her emphasis on "all" pointed at Haley.

Haley looked up at me, and heaved himself from his chair. "Mrs. Buchanan," he said, with no humor left in his voice, "both you and Dr. Whitman are in for unpleasant news at best. Dr. Farraday and I was run off the river road early in the week by a drunken teamster. I cracked my knee, but Doc's dead."

The old woman looked searchingly at Haley, and knew it was no prank. "My soul," she said in a whisper. "How . . ."

"Like I said, we was run off the road. A damn dumb accident. We was goin' out to help Benny Pepper after he got himself shot by his brother. Doc never knew what hit him."

Florence Buchanan's heart beat a time or two in remorse for Farraday and Benny Pepper, then her concern turned to the living. She looked up the street in the direction Whitman had gone. "Then Dr. Whitman doesn't know. I gave him directions to find Dr. Farraday's office, just assuming . . . Oh my stars. And . . ." her voice faded again, "he said that they were so close . . . almost like brothers."

"You get yourself out of the sun, Miz Buchanan. If Patrick here will lend a hand, we'll go up and talk with Dr. Whitman. Might as well be us that brings the bad news."

Mitchell Whitman stood at the bottom of the steps, looking at the sign that pointed up to Farraday's second-floor office and apartment. He smiled to himself and hefted the valise, toying with whether or not to take it to the landing above, where he would knock on the door, wait a respectable time for an answer, and then begin polite inquiries. After a brief pause, he began the climb up the steep stairs, stopping finally in front of the rather plain door with the frosted glass and the simple hand-painted letters announcing the office of John M. Farraday, M.D. Setting down his valise by the door, Whitman rapped loudly, saying loudly as he tried the knob, "John, it's Mitch. You in there?" When no one answered, Whitman tried the knob again, then repeated his knock. After waiting a few seconds, he turned about, looking impatiently up and down the street, as if he expected Farraday to appear from behind a building at any moment. He stopped when he saw Haley slowly hobbling up the boardwalk toward the office, with me giving an occasional assist.

"Dr. Whitman?" Haley stopped at the base of the stairs, both hands on the rail, taking weight off his throbbing knee.

"Yes, indeed." The voice was hearty for such a slight frame. Whitman came down the stairs, leaving his valise at the top. "And I have the pleasure of addressing . . . ?"

"Milt Haley, village marshal. This here," he nodded toward me, "is Patrick Bassett, newspaper." It was a trait of Haley's not to give out more information than he had to, particularly to strangers.

Whitman nodded slightly and extended his hand formally. "As I said, a pleasure." He was younger than he had first appeared getting off the coach, and a little grimier, but stage travel rarely brings out the best in anybody. "Perhaps you can either tell me where I can find Dr. John Farraday, or else direct me toward a spot that serves a good beer while I wait for his return."

"I understand from Miz Buchanan that you're his cousin," Haley said bluntly. He didn't seem in any hurry to deliver the bad news. Whitman flashed a toothy smile.

"Wonderful woman, particularly for her age. The pleasure of her company on the stage was a delight. But yes, I am John's cousin." Whitman leaned on the name "John" as if he were making his privilege of a first-name-basis perfectly clear to us. He stretched to his full height and looked off into the distance. "He said there was considerable opportunity in this valley."

"Indeed," Haley said, and I was amused both at the marshal's use of a word so foreign to his vocabulary and at his so thinly veiled dislike of Whitman. I didn't like the man much myself, although after such short acquaintance I scarcely could have told anyone why. Haley shifted his weight and looked at the ground. "Yep, right now, the nearest doc for this town is back down in Fort Bridger. And that's a two-day hard ride."

"Other than John, you mean," Whitman corrected quickly.

"Well, now that's what we came to tell you, and I'm sorry it's my job. Your cousin, Doc Farraday, well, he got himself killed Monday. I'm sorry there was no way of letting you know before, but as I guess you can understand, things was pretty tight. And we didn't even know he had a cousin. Didn't know he had any relatives at all, matter of fact."

Whitman looked stunned. "Killed? But I don't believe that. I had a last wire from him no more than a week ago, when I was in Denver."

"As I said, it just happened Monday. Him and me was on

a fast run out to one of the ranches where a boy had got himself shot. Freight wagon run us off the road into the river. I banged up my knee, but ole Doc wound up with a busted neck. Funeral was yesterday. Like I said, we had no way of knowin' you'd be here today."

"No, no, I understand now," Whitman said, almost apologetically. "It's just that it's so unexpected. Of course, I would have come earlier if I'd known. Such a tragedy."

Haley straightened up. "El Grande across the way is probably the easiest place for you to stay until you get your bearings."

"Thank you," Whitman replied. He turned for the stairs. "I'd best get my bag. And thank you, Marshal." He paused, looking down at Haley's swollen knee, obvious even under the heavy trousers. "And perhaps it is fortuitous I came anyway. Perhaps I can help that leg some."

"That would be worth payin' for, Dr. Whitman. But you've had a long ride, and my knee can wait. If there's anything else we can do, you just let us know."

I had never heard Haley so solicitous, and it just didn't sound right. I mean, it probably sounded just fine to Whitman, but he didn't know Haley like I did. Other things bothered me too. Docs are used to death, all right, but Dr. Whitman just didn't seem genuinely surprised to find he was short one cousin.

CHAPTER 3

In the two days before he arrived in Ludlum, Mitchell Whitman had been a busy man. News of John Farraday's death had gone to Bridger first through Haley's telegram and second through the arrival of Bud Brown and the arrested freight driver. That news had been a delight for Whitman, and his plans took shape quickly.

After an hour or two spent attending to details, he had drafted a telegram, sent it to Tulsa, Oklahoma, and then purchased a ticket for the northbound stage to Ludlum.

The telegram clicked over the wires to Tulsa, and an earnest young man delivered the message to the office of Dr. Marc Carr. The office of Dr. Carr was in reality nothing more than a first-floor room in the Branding Iron Hotel on Depot Street.

In the light of a kerosene lantern, Marc Carr read the telegram and smiled widely. The lantern light danced across his wide face and startling blue eyes as he read. He turned to the young woman at his side, a woman who at twenty-one was scarcely two years younger than himself.

"Mitch has it all figured out," he said, and his voice was soft. "Seems there's a town north of Fort Bridger that's got no doctor. He says it's small, but easy pickings."

The girl shivered. "Fort Bridger? Isn't that in the Wyoming mountains?"

Carr laughed and put the telegram down. "No, it's not in the mountains, but close enough. Mitch says that by the

51341

time we finish up here, he'll be ready to meet us at the railhead north of Bridger with the list. Then we'll go on up to this Ludlum place by stage and he'll head on west to Evanston, Wyoming."

The girl looked worried and nestled her head against Carr's shoulder. "How many more times are we going to do this, Marc?"

Carr ran his fingers through Alice Lindsay's dark brown hair and then held her head so he was looking directly into her eyes.

"You want to quit?" he asked, his voice nearly a whisper. There was a long pause until the girl spoke again.

"No, I guess not, as long as you know what you're doing." She sighed. "I just want to be in San Francisco by winter, that's all."

Carr stepped away and picked up the telegram again. "We'll be there, all right. I always thought that some of these mountain mining towns would be the easiest of all. Mitch says this one's an easy shot."

"I just hope he's right," the girl said.

"I know he's right, and I'm right. Besides, San Francisco's no fun unless you get there with some gold in your pocket."

The girl laughed dryly. "I trust you, Marc, but I just pray that none of these 'easy shot' towns ever catches you two before you have the chance to light out. If they do, Dr. Carr, it will take more gold than we've got to save your hides."

Carr looked at the girl thoughtfully. "You sound as if you don't have a part in all this," he said. "They'll put you on a rail just as quick as us, so best you have some confidence in what we're about."

Alice Lindsay dropped her gaze and asked quickly, as if to change the subject from something painful, "When do we leave Tulsa?"

"Mitch says to meet him in six days at the railhead north of Fort Bridger. He'll give us the list, and we'll be all set."

"I hope you're right."

"Hey," Carr said suddenly. "Isn't our run here going just fine? Two more days and we'll be on the train bound for Bridger, and we'll be maybe four hundred dollars richer, too. To me, that makes just about anything worth it."

For the first time, Alice Lindsay smiled in agreement. "That's more money than I've seen in a long time," she said. "And I've got to admit, it's all been kinda fun. I just hope . . ." and she hesitated.

"Yes?"

"I just hope we don't get caught." She looked up at Carr. "We won't get caught, will we?"

He put his arm around her shoulders and drew her close. "Nope, we won't. You can always tell when someone's getting curious, and by that time, we'll be long gone. Like Mitch says, Ludlum's a small town, but just the same, we don't have a thing to worry about. We won't get caught."

From the moment Mitchell Whitman arrived in Ludlum, he began building an enviable reputation. Haley still held to his reservations about the "little eastern dude," but few others shared his opinion.

Late Friday afternoon, when Whitman had been in town scarcely more than twenty-four hours, Mrs. Buchanan had bustled into the office of the Ludlum *Herald* and let it be known in no uncertain terms that she expected a fine story and endorsement of the town's new physician in the next edition of the paper. I was tempted to mention that the ink on Farraday's obituary was hardly dry, but refrained.

"I mean, it's so refreshing," she bubbled, her ancient voice nearly cracking with pleasure, "here's a medical man who isn't afraid to admit that maybe he just doesn't know everything in the world." Before I had a chance to say a word, Mrs. Buchanan laid a wrinkled hand on my sleeve. "And he was so embarrassed when he wanted to tell me that maybe my back just hurt because I was . . ." and she paused dramatically, ". . . so old." She cackled gleefully. "He was so polite that he just couldn't bring himself to say it."

I related Mrs. Buchanan's enthusiasm to Marshal Haley later that evening over a beer at the El Grande, but Haley seemed unimpressed. "I just got a feelin', that's all," he said cryptically.

"Well, hell," I replied, "let him have a look-see at that knee of yours. Maybe he'll convince you. Or if you won't do that, take the stage down to Bridger and let the army doc look at it."

"Oh no," Haley said emphatically, unconsciously running his hand protectively over the swollen joint, "ain't no battlefield butcher goin' to cut on me."

"Dr. Farraday was an army doctor before he came here," I reminded the marshal.

Haley was suddenly subdued. "Well, Patrick, that's so, but he was different."

I shook my head. "You can be mighty bullheaded when you want to be. Can't see how you can take your pay when you can't even walk across the street normal-like. You're going to have to do something, and soon at that. If you won't go to Bridger, Whitman's the only doc we got, like him or not."

Haley cursed by way of answer, and downed the rest of his beer.

And like it or not, on Saturday morning Marshal Milt Haley painfully hauled himself up the steps to the office Mitchell Whitman had taken over. At the top of the stairs, he stopped to catch his breath and noticed that Dr. Whitman hadn't removed John Farraday's name from the door. Haley stepped inside, into the front room of a double suite that Farraday had taken great pains in establishing.

Whitman stuck his head around the partition and nodded at Haley. "Be right with you, Marshal. Got a gal here with the grippe." Haley sat down on a straight-back chair, tried to make himself comfortable, and waited. A few moments later, he heard footsteps from behind the partition and looked up, surprised to see Paul and Jody Burton, with Jody supported on one elbow by a pale and sweaty Paul and on the other elbow by Whitman. The doctor's face was concerned, and he was obviously nervous. But it was Jody Burton that drew Haley's attention.

Her eyes were closed, and she walked as if her legs took no commands from her. Her brow was tightly knit, and her hands hung from her wrists as if missing all attachments but the outermost layer of skin. Despite his bad knee, Haley was instantly on his feet, and he held the door for the trio, watching Burton and Whitman carry the nearly unconscious woman down the stairs.

"Now remember," he heard Whitman say as Burton slowly climbed up into the wagon after Jody was settled in the straw in the back, "if she doesn't improve, you just holler. Don't bring her into town again. I'll come out. You shouldn't have brought her in this time. And see if you can get her to take some of that medicine every three hours or so."

He heard Burton mutter something, and then Whitman came back up the stairs. He looked quickly at Haley, saying as he brushed past him into the office, "That's one sick lady. Got a case of the flu that won't quit, I guess."

"She looked awful, all right," Haley said. "Paul didn't look much better."

"Oh, you know them?"

"Sure. Ain't many in this valley I don't know."

Whitman smiled to acknowledge his own ignorance. "I suppose that would be right. I guess my cousin paid a call on them last week, just before he was killed. At least, that's what Mr. Burton says. Apparently his wife is no better, and he got worried and brought her into town. Anyway," he said, changing the subject abruptly, "let's look at that knee."

Haley winced involuntarily as Whitman ran a hand down the side of his swollen knee. After a brief examination, Whitman leaned back in his chair. "Well, Marshal, as I see it, you've got two choices. You can either go to Fort Bridger, or wherever else there's a qualified surgeon, or you can continue to stumble around town here until maybe this thing gets better."

The marshal drew his trouser leg back down. "And how long you figure that 'maybe' will be?"

Whitman shrugged. "Don't know. For a joint to be that swollen, has to be something pretty wrong inside. Anybody can see that. Whether it'll heal properly or not would just be a guess on my part."

Haley looked steadily at Whitman, and their eyes met.

"Then guess," Haley said flatly. "I ain't goin' to have it cut on."

Whitman got up and walked to his large satchel on the desk. "I won't play games with you, Marshal. I won't guess. Could be a week, could be the rest of your life." He rummaged through the satchel. "All I can do is give you something to help the pain, and suggest further that you rest as much as possible." He removed a small phial from the case and squinted at the label, then put it back and selected another and handed it to Haley. "Try this."

Haley scrutinized the bottle of Dr. Punget's Joint and Limb Tonic. "This help?"

Whitman leaned against the table and smiled. "Probably not."

Haley took out the cork and sniffed, then took a tentative taste. His eyebrows went up. "Not bad, what's in it?"

"Cheap whiskey."

Haley was momentarily taken aback by Whitman's bald-faced answer, and his face showed his astonishment.

"Not all medicine is whiskey," Whitman said smoothly, "but a good deal is nothing more than alcohol. Right now, that's about all I can give you to help ease whatever pain you might have. The sample's free, if you want it. If you need more, I suggest you visit the El Grande as often as needed. Like I said, you need a surgeon. I'd be a liar if I told you anything else."

Haley hobbled to his feet and extended his hand. "Doc, you're an honest man. I didn't like you when we first met, but I kinda think we might understand each other." He handed back the bottle of Dr. Punget's. "You keep this. I can buy my own." He hesitated. "By the way, you tell everyone that what you give them is nothing more than bar traffic?"

Whitman smiled quickly. "No, and I don't give it to everyone, either. But sometimes, in a few cases, just what someone believes they're getting does the most good." He winked at Haley. "Don't give away my secrets."

"You can count on it, Doc." He opened the door. "I owe you anything?"

The man in the office shrugged. "I didn't do anything for you. But next time"—and he chuckled—"I'll really clip ya to make up for this visit."

Whitman continued to see patients that day, went to church Sunday, tipped his hat to every new prospective patient he met, and was hard at work Monday morning. He treated, talked, cajoled all morning—but mostly, it seemed, he listened—listened with care to every complaint and symptom, real or imagined. He ate a hearty lunch at the El Grande, and before the telegram arrived in mid-afternoon, Whitman had "seen" four more patients. Ralph Kressen came in shortly after noon with a badly sliced palm earned after a piece of coiled barbed wire got away from him. Fearful of the number of stitches the wound would take, he was greatly relieved when Whitman pshawed the need and washed the wound liberally with whiskey and applied a loose bandage. "Keep it clean," he told Kressen, and collected a ten-dollar gold piece. The rancher was so glad not to be sewed up that he paid without hesitation.

No more than fifteen minutes after Kressen left, Mrs. Buchanan's best friend, Bertha Sillitoe, an overweight woman of sixty-odd years, panted her way up the stairs, her overworked heart thumping dangerously in her ears. Whitman listened carefully and took copious notes while Mrs. Sillitoe ran through her entire and lengthy medical history, charged her five dollars and saw her out the door with a small bottle labeled "Dr. Rothfuss' Heart Elixir" and cautious advice to "take it easy and avoid red meats." Mrs. Sillitoe liked a good steak, and this advice that went so contrary to her own dietary inclinations struck her as profound and certainly serious. She was greatly pleased and stopped off on her way home to tell a friend about her new forced abstinence.

After a break to enjoy a small cigar, Whitman was back at work a few moments later. Even as a man with no medical training, he could guess that Mrs. Bonitis' eleven-month-old child was probably bouncing-baby healthy, its fat pink cheeks ripe with all things good. But Mrs. Bonitis insisted that the child was fretful and needed attention. Whitman remembered something his now deceased but formerly very wise aunt had told his mother as she rocked his youngest brother—a brother who would not sleep unless the room was pitch-dark. Remembering the words nearly verbatim, he repeated them to Mrs. Bonitis.

"Some infants are day-sleepers, Mrs. Bonitis, and some are night-sleepers, and some, praise the Lord, are both. Those that aren't are too young to change their way of thinking, so us tired old parents have to make the change instead."

"You mean I should just let him stay awake during the day?" the mother asked incredulously.

"If he won't sleep, you can rock and croon from now till doomsday. Just ignore him and before you know it, he'll decide when he's tuckered and just fall asleep."

Mrs. Bonitis looked down at the happy infant, who was playing with the end of a stethoscope that formerly had belonged to John Farraday but now hung from Whitman's neck. The infant looked up, focused on Whitman's face, and gurgled, breaking down Mrs. Bonitis' last resistance. She paid Whitman five dollars and left, happier with her wakeful infant. Whitman was happy to see them go. He didn't like treating children—they were difficult to bluff.

His last visit of the day came from three highly distraught men and one who was beyond emotion. Louis White had been careless, picking a damp patch of earth to slip on just as an eight-horse team pulling a two-ton skid of logs passed. The logs had crushed White's right leg to a shapeless pulp, and the logger had bled to death before his friends could get a wagon to town. Whitman looked at the dead man briefly, listened perfunctorily with the stethoscope to make sure White was dead, and directed the three to take the body to the funeral parlor just a convenient block down the street.

Whitman had barely enough time to catch his breath when the delivery boy from the telegraph office at the end of the street ran up the stairs and handed over the message Whitman had been waiting for. Feigning a look of surprise, he unfolded the paper and read the brief message quickly. "I've just lost my father," he said sadly for the boy's benefit, and handed the youth a penny, even though the boy obviously didn't want reimbursement as the bearer of bad news.

The telegram was actually from Carr, who along with Alice Lindsay was on the train from Tulsa, and now only a day out of Bridger. The message about Whitman's fictitious father was the prearranged excuse Whitman needed to leave town without causing suspicion. With a funeral in San Francisco, there was no telling how long the new doctor would be gone. The people whom Whitman had entertained during the course of his brief stay in Ludlum didn't know, as he boarded the stage the next day, that they would never see him again.

But quickly enough, they would begin to rely on a fresh-faced new doctor in town—a physician who would arrive by stage in company with his attractive nurse-sister only two days after Whitman's departure.

The town so masterfully set up by Whitman would be easy pickings for Marc Carr and the girl he intended to marry later that year in San Francisco. Before the couple left the railhead for Ludlum, Whitman would hand deliver his carefully kept list of patients and their ailments—many of those patients were no more than lonely hypochondriacs looking for a sympathetic ear—and armed with that list, Carr would appear to be a most perceptive physician indeed . . . until he and his "nurse" would also slip away from Ludlum, their pockets full of easy money. The scheme had worked successfully in several other towns, most, like Tulsa, considerably larger than Ludlum. Whitman would take the train west to Evanston, Wyoming Territory, preparing that town as the next target while Carr and Lindsay picked Ludlum clean. The small town on the Little Muddy River seemed an especially easy mark. But Jody Burton had changed all that.

CHAPTER 4

Paul Burton was not especially bright, but he knew two things for certain. He knew that his wife was probably dying, and he knew that he himself was desperately ill. When Farraday had visited nearly two weeks ago, he had not said much, but Burton had been able to tell that the doctor was worried. Farraday had asked about the milk that they drank every day and had even walked to the spring, returning with a frown. He had said that he needed more medicine and left, promising to return before the day was over. After that, there had been no doctor for the Burtons.

Jody had complained of a persistent headache, when she complained at all, but now she lay silently, occasionally tossing in a semicoma. Back from the trip into town to see Whitman, Burton, himself ill to the point where willpower alone drove him about the small house, had tried to keep at least the bed in order but soon failed even in that. Lacking the physical power to do anything to help either himself or his wife, he had stopped noticing, after a day or two, the stench in the house from the diarrhea, and the last things he remembered hearing before collapsing into a chair beside the bed were his wife's soft moanings drifting only occasionally across the room, and the distant and plaintive nicker of one of the horses. The last of the medicine from Dr. Whitman, obtained during the visit to town now nearly a week ago, was long gone.

The Burtons' neighbor Randy Kane found the couple

early in the morning. He had known that the Burtons were sick, having met them on the road as they drove in to see the new physician. But matters had kept him from stopping by the ranch for a week. What he found that morning when he did visit sent him outside into the bushes. When no one answered his knock, he had pushed the door gently and found it open. Paul Burton was unconscious in the chair, with his wife curled tightly on her side in the bed. The small house stank heavily, and Kane opened every window that would move, letting in the cool evening air. The jolt of fresh air seemed to make the smell even worse, and Kane had to retreat outside until his stomach was emptied and stopped churning. When he went back inside, he found Paul Burton more or less awake, his eyes dull and listless.

"My God, man, what is it?" he asked, and Paul stared up at him for long seconds, as if it took his fevered brain that long to recognize Kane. Finally he spoke, and his voice was dry and small, almost as if his tongue would not follow the feeble directions from the brain.

"Fix the bed, would you, Randy?" The eyes pleaded up at him through their dullness, and Kane, without looking over at the horror of the bed, nodded. "And check the stock?"

"Sure, Paul, sure. You don't worry about nothin'. And after I get you all sorta comfortable, I'll ride into town and see if the doc can come out." He went over to the bed, wondering if the woman, pale and still, was dead. He pulled off the quilt, and trying to force himself to ignore the mess that an unconscious patient with no tending makes, looked hard at Jody. He could see her chest moving up and down with rapid inhalations, and he breathed a sigh of relief that she was still alive. Moving awkwardly, he slid her to one side of the bed and yanked off the soiled linens, tossing them in a heap by the door. The bedclothes she was wearing consisted only of a long nightshirt that obviously belonged to Paul.

That too was soiled, but Kane was out of his element. He had gone far enough without changing the woman's clothes as well, particularly with the husband in the same room.

"You got any more beddin'?" he asked Paul, but Burton had once more slipped from consciousness. Kane stood, feeling embarrassed and useless. He went to a closet where he had seen Jody put fresh-dried wash before and opened the door. There was another heap of bedding on the floor of the closet, not nearly as soiled as that which he had removed, but still not clean enough. Even Kane recognized that. He stood for a moment, then slammed the closet door.

"Well, goddamn it, then, I'll just rinse out this stuff in the crick. At least that way they'll have something in a couple hours." He grabbed the linen from the closet and the other linen he had just removed from the bed and quietly left the house.

Ghost Creek had slowed somewhat but still was running full after the recent rain. Kane found a relatively slow-moving pool and rinsed the soiled linens, one piece at a time, until he was sure that they would dry acceptably clean. Trudging back to the house with the wrung-out bedding, he went around back and hung the linen on the clothesline. "Make somebody a good wife," he muttered, and returned to the house. Burton was still unconscious, but Jody was tossing and turning on the linenless bed. Kane slipped a blanket over her and backed away. "God, you folks really got it," he murmured, and left the house.

The horses, despite the days of no attention, had fared all right, though they were hungry and nervous. Kane tossed in hay, then walked quickly to the barn. After only a moment he came out and fetched his rifle from his saddle. The report was achingly loud when it came, and then Kane emerged again, head down. He swung up on his horse and galloped off as hard as he could toward Ludlum.

The day before Randy Kane galloped his horse to a lather anxiously seeking help for his neighbors, Marc Carr and Alice Lindsay arrived in the village. They came by stage, early enough in the day to find a suitable storefront for an office.

Both Milt Haley and I had met the couple and were impressed with their earnestness. The young man and his "sister" were a model couple. Dr. Carr had firmly refused the offer of Farraday's old office, even with Whitman gone for an indeterminate time, saying that it wouldn't be "proper" to take advantage of an estate before the relatives had their chance—however long that took. Instead, he accepted a generous offer from Homer Woodstock for the use of a large side room of the mercantile—a room that fronted not only on the main street but that bounded the side alley as well.

The arrival of the young doctor and his nurse sister was cause for considerable high spirits in Ludlum. Whitman had immediately filled the void left by Farraday's death, and the second man's departure only had increased the town's sense of unpreparedness for the winter. With Carr's arrival, hopes flew sky-high again. This man, obviously a young and bright physician, was looking for a small town in which to settle. The folks of Ludlum would be more than hospitable. And, said the hearts of those who had time to discourse on such things, both Carr and his sister Alice were unmarried. Double-barreled speculation would help fill the long, late winter days, to bloom with spring.

Further, in a country already accustomed to such things, it was obvious the young doctor and his nurse were hard workers. Hadn't they eschewed an office already established and equipped to make it on their own?

"We'll work up to what we need," Carr told me the afternoon of his arrival in Ludlum, when Haley, myself, and

even "sort-of-mayor" Herb Allen tried to convince him to
take over the office.

So, the couple rented a pair of adjoining rooms, inexpen-
sive but suitable, on the second floor of the El Grande and
went right to work, straightening out the new office just
across the street, arranging some furniture that Woodstock,
the landlord, offered for their use. I could see right off that
there was plenty of "working up" for that young couple.
They came with no more than Carr's large black medical
bag, and two valises—not much to start a practice on . . .
and with the rate we got deliveries from outside the valley, I
was plainly worried that the building of Carr's office would
proceed at a pace a good deal less than slowly.

From Carr's viewpoint, on the other hand, progress was
phenomenal. He knew from experience that Whitman had a
keen eye for assessing a situation, but Ludlum was a gold
mine. The evening of his arrival in Ludlum, Carr settled
back on the edge of the narrow bed of his room and took the
list Whitman had compiled, looking at each name and description carefully.

"Would you look at this, Alice?" His fiancée raised her
head off the pillow slightly. She was stretched out beside
Carr. "Whitman was here for only a few days, yet he's got,
let's see," and he counted aloud, tapping each name with his
index finger, "thirty-three people here."

"So what does that mean?" Alice asked sleepily.

"Come on, gal. Remember Tulsa? We plucked forty
there. This place is no more than one side of one street of
Tulsa, and yet he got us maybe thirty. We get even half of
that, and a hundred fifty, two, maybe even three hundred
dollars, and from a two-bit town like this. Hell, from what
Whitman says, there isn't a doctor within thirty or forty
miles of here."

He fell silent again, reading the list. Whitman had been a

careful listener, all right. After each patient's name was a thorough compilation of all mentioned symptoms, real or imaginary. After five or six names he had written, "real sick," but most of the names represented nothing more than frontier hypochondriacs—folks with time on their hands and vivid imaginations to listen to each metabolic stirring in their bodies and call it part of some dread illness or "condition." They were easy prey, Carr thought happily, and imaginary treatments would be a luxury cheerfully afforded, particularly when those treatments were dispensed by a young and earnest physician. Those patients who were really ill were the greatest worry to Carr. They were to be avoided, or if that was not possible, steered carefully, with the constant hope that nature would take a benign course until he was out of town. In large cities, they could be sent to other physicians who didn't know the newcomers' credentials and who wouldn't question the referral.

Carr read Whitman's notes after Bertha Sillitoe's name and chuckled. He knew what he would say to the elderly woman already, and he knew a guaranteed success when he saw one. Milt Haley's name caught his eye, and he read carefully Whitman's notes on the stumpy marshal.

"Marshal's got a bum knee," he mused aloud. "We won't have to worry about outrunning him."

"What did Mitchell do for him?" Alice asked, and raised herself up on one elbow. She was a pretty girl, with long dark hair that she usually kept tied in a bun at the back of her head. She had met Carr in Cambridge when he was a sophomore and in the last year he had studied at Harvard, and she had been drawn by the fire of the young man, drawn by his rebellious nature, drawn by his persistent desire to see "the other side" of the country. She had not liked his friends, primarily Mitchell Whitman, and she had not particularly liked the way the two men talked intently late into the night. But a year after she met him, she did like his plan to go to San Francisco, and with delight she abandoned a tedious job in a clothing factory. Ludlum was more than two-thirds of the way to their dream. Her parents, mildly scandalized at her traveling unchaperoned with young Carr, knew nothing of the route being taken.

"It says here," said Carr, holding the page so that more light fell on the paper, "that he told the marshal to go to a surgeon, that he couldn't do anything about it. Told him to drink whiskey for the pain." Carr laughed shortly. "Says he told Haley that a lot of the elixirs are nothing but whiskey." He lowered his voice a notch. "Also says that we should be careful, that Haley's 'smart.'" He read on in silence, and his eye was caught by what Whitman had written about the Burtons.

Alice saw his forehead wrinkle. "What's wrong," she asked.

Carr looked up quickly, then back at the paper. "Nothing, I guess. Whitman says that some folks named Burton are probably pretty sick. Doesn't know what, but says we should avoid them if we can." He scanned on down the list. "Other than a couple injuries, it looks like that's about it." He folded the paper carefully. "I guess we can handle it all right."

But the next morning, after their first breakfast in Ludlum, their ability to "handle it" received its first test when Randy Kane galloped into town for help.

CHAPTER 5

Jane Hexley's Romance isn't really all that exciting—I was sure that nearly everyone reading it knew that Lord Smith-Wraight would soften up in the end and a joyous matrimony would be enjoyed by all. Still, if I had stopped running the installments, I probably would have been lynched.

What did bother me was the way Jim Flower had to laboriously read the darn thing through before he started to set the type. I came up behind him and reached over his shoulder, putting a finger on the first word of the first paragraph.

"See, if you start right here," I said, "you'll be in the right place. I gather that's what you're doing, looking for the right place to start."

Jim looked up at me, his face blank, then understood. "Yeah," he said foolishly. "I got carried away readin'. I'll have it done by this afternoon."

I patted Flower on the shoulder. "That and a whole lot more besides, I hope. Next Tuesday is just around the corner, you know."

"But we was late last week," Flower protested. "Ain't we goin' to be late this week too?"

I laughed. "Jim," I explained patiently, "the fact that we came out late last week doesn't mean that we're going to change our press day from now on. What it does mean is that this week is like any other week, and as usual, we're both behind. And that means that you need to step up the pace a little."

"Oh, yeah," he said, as if the entire situation had finally dawned on him. Sometimes I wondered how Flower ever got up enough gumption to learn to read. But, like I said, he didn't give me any yap.

I turned and looked out the dirty window at the bright sun, and looked across the street just in time to see Randy Kane dismount in front of Farraday's office steps. He bounded up them three at a time, and I watched him as he stood at the door, impatiently waiting for an answer. I'm naturally nosey, so I stepped out of my office—a location I take pride in, since I can see virtually every building in Ludlum from the slight rise occupied by the slab-board structure that houses the *Herald*—and called over to Kane.

"Who you after, Randy?"

Kane for a minute didn't register the direction of my voice, and he twisted and turned, finally looking nearly straight down from the landing, as if I was in the alley.

"Across the street," I yelled at him, and he finally saw me. He raised a hand and came down the stairs the same way he went up, three at a time, and ran across the street to where I stood.

"Where's Whitman?" he asked between gasps for breath.

"Whitman? You mean Doc Whitman?" Kane nodded. "Hell," I said, "he had to leave town for San Francisco. Left Tuesday on the stage."

Kane shook his head like it didn't matter if Whitman had left or not. "Well, he's needed. The Burtons is awful sick. Never saw nothin' like it. I think she's dyin', and Paul ain't much better off."

"Well, then," I replied, and I still remember what I said, word for word, "they're lucky folks, all right." I told Kane about the new doctor in town. "Dr. Carr is settin' up his office over on the side of Woodstock's store, and that's where you'll find him, no doubt. If he's not there, try the El Grande . . . that's where him and his sister the nurse are staying." I stepped off the porch. "Come on, I'll introduce you to 'em."

Dr. Carr was indeed in his new office, such as it was. The only furnishings were a large desk, two chairs, and a folding screen that Woodstock had lent them, put to use in separating part of the room for an examining area. The doctor's sister was dressed in a reasonably white long dress, and with a white kerchief on her head. A tribute to the success of their undertaking was embodied at the moment in the presence of Bertha Sillitoe, who, although she had rejoiced in the attention of Dr. Whitman, had found the strictures of his no-meat recommendations too burdensome—after less than a week. Now she had turned to this fresh, young physician for further guidance.

But Dr. Carr was a good deal more firm than Whitman. When Mrs. Sillitoe had entered the office, the young physician had hardly allowed her two words. He had listened to her heart with a cold-belled stethoscope while his nurse stood silently and prettily at his side. Mrs. Sillitoe had felt awed. After listening for a full minute, Dr. Carr had stood up straight and fastened the elderly woman with a hard and serious look.

"Now, my good woman, let me see if I understand you," he had said, even though Mrs. Sillitoe had uttered hardly a word that needed understanding. "At the risk of being indelicate, I would assume first of all that Dr. Farraday was treating you for a bad heart."

Mrs. Sillitoe nodded sagely. "Why, yes, he was, and . . ."

Before she could finish, Carr had continued his recitation of everything he knew about the woman. "And you suffer frequently from dizzy spells, don't you?" And again before she could answer, he had plunged on. "You frequently have to stop even very minor exertion in order to catch your breath. There are nights when you don't sleep well. Even in summer, your feet seem frozen to the bone." He had hesitated long enough to glance at the nurse, as if to indicate that the presence of another woman in the room acted as a tempering agent. "And your ankles sometimes swell, don't they?" Mrs. Sillitoe was astounded at such an accurate description of her endless ailments, exactly what Whitman had gleaned by merely letting the woman prattle on. All the information on Mrs. Sillitoe was on the list, and Carr knew the list well.

"If I may be so rude," Carr had continued, smiling broadly, "most of your condition can be remedied by taking off about fifty or sixty pounds." He chuckled at Mrs. Sillitoe's sudden intake of breath, and patted her affectionately on the hand. "I know that's a lot to ask, but your health would improve to a degree where you would be a new person. And with winter coming on, you know the rigors of the season."

By now, Mrs. Sillitoe was meekly at the doctor's mercy. As we came into the office, he was finishing his prescription. "I would endorse Dr. Whitman's suggestion that you avoid red meats. They do the heart no good. I would further insist that you begin to restrict your consumption of fatty foods by about half. Alice, would you fetch me some of Dr. Goodson's Circulation Restorer?" He continued with Mrs. Sillitoe, while Kane and I waited patiently on the other side of the screen. "If the strictures of the diet become unbearable, or if you begin to feel either weak or somewhat dizzy, take a tablespoon or two of Dr. Goodson's. It will surely help." He took the bottle from his nurse and handed it to Mrs. Sillitoe. "You need to take care of yourself, my dear," he said solicitously. "Perhaps you should check with me again next week, and we'll see what progress you're making."

I noticed that Carr already had a bill prepared, and his nurse handed it to Mrs. Sillitoe as she gathered her wrap. The elderly woman's eyes shot up at what was obviously a substantial figure. "Mercy," she said aloud. Dr. Carr again smiled his wide and charming smile.

"Yes, ill health is far more costly than good health. But we hope to have you on the right road very shortly."

Mrs. Sillitoe dug into her satchel and paid, but from where we were standing by the door, I could not tell the extent of the bill. As she walked past us to the door, after murmuring a somewhat contrite sounding thank-you to Dr. Carr and the nurse, she was tightly clutching the pint bottle of Dr. Goodson's, and her eyes were shining with pleasure. Doctoring that caused pain in the pocketbook must have caused her considerable pleasure in the heart.

"Gentlemen!" Carr boomed out loudly, striding up to us. He reached out and pumped my hand. "Ah, Mr. . . . ah, . . . Bassett? . . . is it?"

I nodded. "This here is Randy Kane, from up just north of town. He just came into town looking for Doc Whitman, but of course, he isn't here anymore. So I told him he best come see you."

Carr looked politely interested and shook Kane's hand. "And what may I do for you, Mr. Kane?"

Kane had cooled off some, but he was still excited. "It's the Burtons," he said. "I just left their place. They needja, Doc. God almighty, but they're sick. She looked like she was fixin' to die, and he sure didn't look much better. Whole place smells terrible."

Dr. Carr hesitated and looked at his nurse, who stood quietly by the desk. "Let me see who all I expect this afternoon," he said, and walked to the desk, opening a ledger.

We waited impatiently while he read in the book, then looked at a folded paper that he had kept under the front leaf of the ledger. Finally he looked up and addressed Kane. "Do you suppose they would be able to wait until tomorrow?"

Kane shook his head vehemently, and Carr spoke again. "No, I suppose not." He sighed. "How far is it?"

"Less than a mile," Kane said quickly.

"I don't have a horse," Carr said, equally quickly, and I was beginning to feel uneasy.

I said, "You're welcome to use my buckboard. Not fancy, but it will get you there." Carr was suddenly all efficiency.

"Good." He turned to his nurse, who had not uttered a word during the entire time we had been in the office. "Alice, you stay here in case someone comes. You can tell them where I am and that I'll be back before long. If it's something simple, you give them what they need." He turned back to us. "Shall we go, then?" With satchel in hand, he followed us out the door. Kane took his own mount and went on ahead while I rigged my own sorrel, Gert, to the buckboard. Before long, we were headed out of the village, driving north along the narrow road that led away from the Little Muddy, up along the Ghost Creek cut, toward the few settlements that lay up the valley. For the first few moments, Dr. Carr was silent, then he turned to me and said, "I understand that you run the local newspaper here."

I nodded. I was always proud of the *Herald*, even when there was no news in it, which was most of the time. "Yes, me and that newspaper have been here in Ludlum for almost seven years."

"That must be quite a challenge," Carr observed.

"It could be," I laughed. "But I retired from the big city papers back East. Got left an inheritance and decided to 'get away from it all,' and came here. I sure got away from it.

But I don't take it too seriously anymore. I guess you could say I do the paper more for fun than anything else. I don't hold presstimes too all god-awful important, and I got me pretty good and cheap help. What I do most of the time is just enjoy myself."

"In Ludlum?" Carr asked, obviously skeptical, and I was surprised.

I urged Gert into a semblance of eager motion. "Sure. Why not? Great hunting, good fishing, just enough people. Even the weather's interesting, if you keep your sense of humor."

"I see," Carr said. We rounded a slight bend in the rough trail, and I could see Garcia's cabin near the creek bank, perilously close to the edge. "Is that the house?" Carr asked.

"No, that's Garcia's. He helps the Burtons once in a while, otherwise doesn't do much of anything worthwhile. Burton's place is just ahead, but further away from the creek." Not a word was spoken for the remainder of the short trip, but I noticed that Carr seemed nervous, shifting the valise he held close from hand to hand. Once he quickly wiped the palms of his hands on his trousers.

I tapped on the reins as we pulled in front of the Burtons' flat log house, and Gert didn't need any more encouragement to stop. I could see Kane's horse tied beside the house, but Kane was not in sight. Carr and I walked quickly to the front door, and it was opened by Kane, his face in a grimace.

"Same as before," he said. "Jesus, but it stinks in there." He turned and let us past, and the odor of the house hit our noses like a well-directed fist. Paul Burton was stretched out on the bed beside his wife. He was fully dressed, she was in one of his nightshirts, and the mattress was stripped of bedding. I looked around the room quickly for something to throw on the bed, and saw nothing.

"They can't just lie on the bare mattress like that," I said, and Kane quickly answered.

"I washed some linen as best I could earlier. It should be dry by this time. It's out back . . . I'll go get it."

Carr stood at the foot of the bed, the valise still in hand, obviously deep in thought.

"What do you think, Doc?" I asked. Carr shrugged and dropped the valise to the floor by his feet.

"Two obviously very ill people," he said. "Why don't you help your friend there with the bedding. I'll examine these folks and see what's the matter." I couldn't see how a grown man needed help with a couple of linens, but I went outside anyhow, thankful for the fresh air. All in all we stayed at the Burtons' for about an hour. When Kane and I came back inside with the linen, which, although just stream washed, seemed sparkling white compared with the atmosphere inside that cabin, Dr. Carr was finishing up with his examination of Jody Burton. He was talking quietly to her, and to her husband also. His stethoscope hung from around his neck. Although Jody occasionally mumbled, it soon was obvious to me that she was not aware of Carr's presence. Her face was pale, in marked contrast to the horrid darkness of the bed and pillow. As Carr moved around the bed to Paul's side of the bed, I noticed the blood stains on her pillow, and then immediately saw that she had been bleeding from the nose. Carr bent over and spoke with Paul, who lay quietly, his eyes open but glassy. I couldn't hear what he said, but I saw Paul nod weakly and speak in return. Finally Carr straightened up and came over to Kane and me. He spoke softly, indicating the door. We went outside, and the sunshine felt good on our backs after the dark of the cabin.

"They both have quite high fevers," he said, "she more than he, I would guess. Without a more thorough examination, I can't be positive, but I would say that their problem is one of two things, perhaps even both. Obviously they both have severe influenza, but I would also guess that there's been some sort of food poisoning as well. Her abdomen is very tender, and he says that they both have had diarrhea for several days." He paused. "In any case, they need someone here to see after them. She's nearly unconscious, and he is not much better. Is there someone in town who could come out here for a couple of days, put their house together and see to administration of food and medicine?"

Our town didn't have an abundance of trained nurses. At the moment, I couldn't even think of one, except for the doctor's own assistant. I suggested her as a possibility, and Carr quickly demurred.

"No, I need her in the office with me." He smiled quickly. "It can become somewhat, ah, indelicate if she isn't there when women patients are in the office."

"How about Lucy Gardner?" I asked. Kane readily agreed. Lucy Gardner, a widow of sixty-odd years, had served as midwife on innumerable occasions, and her own family of eleven children successfully grown was proof enough that she had plenty of experience managing illness and injury.

"Fine," Carr said. "I've left a plentiful supply of the medicine they need within easy reach. If one of you, or anyone, for that matter, can bring Mrs. Gardner out here, that would help. The sooner the better. That house"—and he turned to look through the door—"needs a thorough cleaning and airing out. Not to mention that bed they're on. That should be burned." Just as he finished speaking, we heard heavy coughing, followed by a piteous moan from inside. "We should waste no more time," Carr said, and strode off toward the buckboard.

I caught Kane by the arm. "I'll see about Mrs. Gardner," I

said. "You've done plenty here. I'm sure you have your own chores at home."

Kane looked thankful, then shook his head. "I'll stop by and tend the horses." He paused. "I shot the cow. She was too far gone, tied all those days untended. I'll drag her off somewhere for the coyotes when I go back." He ran fingers through his thick hair. "You think they'll be all right?" he asked desperately. "Jeez, I ain't never seen anything like that."

"I think so, Randy. But it's a good thing the doc came along when he did. Whitman's leaving kinda left us high and dry."

CHAPTER 6

Late that night, after he had closed his office for the day, Carr poured himself a long drink. He offered the bottle to Alice, who shook her head.

"I think we should leave in the morning," she said firmly. Carr looked at her and laughed.

"Leave? Thirty-five dollars we made today, not even counting all the time I had to take going out to that ranch this morning." He took a sip and grimaced. "You want to give all that up? In a week we could be well on the way."

Alice got up and came to Carr, putting her arms around his neck. She was extremely slender, and Carr held her with one arm, the other supporting his drink. "I know," she said. "You and Mitch have it all figured out how to make all kinds of money. But Marc, this is such a small town. One little slip, and we'll be caught." She looked directly into his eyes for a moment. "You don't know how much that thought scares me, Marc. There's a lot of things I can take, but jail's not one of them."

Carr disengaged himself gently. "Believe me, Ali, we are not going to be caught. What can they do even if we are? We've done more good than harm—we've done no harm, in fact, just fed a few fancies. It's an easy way to make money, and no one's the worse for it." He went to the window and looked out. "We can get to San Francisco with plenty of cash in hand. Maybe go into business for ourselves, maybe buy a store of some kind. Maybe go to Europe."

"Maybe you should study medicine," Alice offered. "Finish your schooling." She moved over to the window to stand beside him. "You've done very well so far. I enjoyed watching you talk with that lady who had the baby."

Carr laughed softly. "Ah, yes. Mrs. Bonitis. She saw Whitman, too. Can't stand it that her baby frets during the day." He shook his head. "Anything to have something to talk about. I wonder what her husband would say about all this. I guess he's away on a cattle drive. But anyway, no, I don't want to study medicine. My father wanted that, you know. For a year or so, I even thought I wanted it, too. I went to Harvard, thinking so, until I realized that I was just trying to keep him happy. But I got tired of that. I get tired of people. And I get tired of caring whether they feel good or bad." Carr sighed. "But the day did go well. Maybe what I should be is a professional actor."

"You are, dear, you are," Alice said, and pinched his arm.

Carr put his arm around the girl, and they both stood quietly, the soft light filtering in through the window and framing their faces in fine shadows.

Whitman had been right, Carr thought. There was more to life than stuffy classrooms, dimly lighted pharmacies cluttered with incomprehensible drugs, and ancient, starch-fronted professors who smelled of embalming fluid. There was more money to be made, and made easily, elsewhere. And it could be made without the years of brain-aching study that the college demanded.

It had been late at night, deep in the fourth, maybe fifth, stein of beer served up in a local Cambridge pub, when Carr had been infected by the contagious spirit of reckless adventure that moved Mitchell Whitman, and Carr found himself caught up in the words of his friend. Although older than Carr, Whitman was also making a futile effort at formal education. Now thoroughly weary of study and impatient to own the world, he found ready ears as he talked to the younger man.

"We can do it," Whitman had said that night. "You remember what old Burgess said?" And he did a passable imitation of Professor Lester Burgess, a venerated don of the college. "'If you gentlemen listen to your patients, their stories will tell you more than any trunkload of medical books.'" Whitman's voice whined higher. "'And understanding is worth more than a roomful of the best pharmaceutica.'" He laughed. "If the old prof is right, we can trade on it, and I know just how."

And he had outlined his scheme then and there, a plan that relied on the basic trust in human nature.

Months later, standing and looking out on the streets of Ludlum, Wyoming Territory, Marc Carr felt a certain satisfaction. He hugged Alice tighter. "And how well it all works," he thought to himself.

While Carr and Miss Lindsay were enjoying each other's company in a way then unimagined by any of the rest of us, I wasn't sure I had volunteered for the right job. It had been late afternoon before Lucy Gardner could go out to the Burtons', and since I had suggested her it fell to me to deliver the goods, as it were. As I sat outside the Burtons' house, resting against the broad trunk of a spruce and smoking my pipe, I could think of a dozen places I would rather have been. Leaning against the spruce rail of the El Grande's bar would have been one choice. I was thirsty. Turning to catch a glimpse of Mrs. Gardner's industry every so often just increased that thirst. I had offered to help. But she had firmly declined, muttering something about men and uselessness. I hadn't pressed the issue. When the sun sank behind the trees, evening and the temperature fell with a vengeance. I got my coat from the buckboard and put it on, turning just in time to see Mrs. Gardner at the doorway. She beckoned me to the house, and when I stepped through the door, I was astounded at the change. The room smelled nearly bearable, the bed was freshly changed, indeed the entire room looked cheerful and airy. She had ripped the covering of the horse-hair mattress off earlier, and I had burned it outside. In its place she had used a clean blanket she had brought with her from town, and then a pad on top of that to absorb whatever unpleasantness might be produced by the two ill occupants of the bed.

No matter how clean the room, however, my concern for the Burtons remained unchanged. Jody was still in a stupor, occasionally opening her eyes to talk with an imaginary audience. Her nose still bled, and Mrs. Gardner had to be alert to save the covering of the pillow. Except for the brief moments of fitfullness, Jody Burton remained in a semicoma, her fever obviously dangerously high, her breathing shallow and rapid. Paul, on the other hand, seemed somewhat improved. He seemed far less frail than Jody even when both were healthy, and obviously the illness that had struck had sought her out more than him. As I came through the door, he lifted his head from the bed and looked at me wanly.

"She's something, ain't she?" he said weakly, indicating Mrs. Gardner. "We sure do thank you." His attention wandered, and then he saw his wife beside him, reacting as if he had noticed her only for the first time. "How's the woman?" he asked, and Mrs. Gardner beat me in answer.

"I think she'll be all right. She seems better already. Now," she continued in an authoritative manner, "I'll be back first thing in the morning. You both will be fine until then." She bustled over to the breadboard, and came back to the bedside with an earthenware pitcher. "Here's some good fresh water, and there's some broth on the stove. I want you to drink as much as you can, but only if you feel up to it.

And if you can get Jody to take some of the medicine that Dr. Carr sent, that would be fine too."

Paul Burton nodded weakly and settled back into the pillow. He took his wife's limp hand in his, and that small act seemed to require nearly all his strength. "We'll be fine now," he said, and closed his eyes.

"I'll be back first light," Mrs. Gardner said cheerfully, and pushed me out the door with surprising strength.

When we were outside, I turned to the energetic woman walking beside me to the buckboard. "Not going to stay the night?" I asked.

Mrs. Gardner snorted. "I should say not. Influenza, indeed." She lurched up into the buckboard and sat down on the rude seat with a hearty thud. She fixed me with an icy glare. "Had I known before we drove out here what the real problem was, I would have come prepared. No, I'll come out tomorrow, and I'll come prepared."

I was taken aback. "What do you mean, 'the real problem'? Didn't Dr. Carr fill you in?"

"Oh, yes," she said airily. "And either young master Carr is a bumbling fool or he thinks that I don't need to know the truth. Honestly." She slapped me on the arm and pointed down the road. "May we get on? I have much to do, and I'm tired."

I urged Gert into motion, but my curiosity would not go unsatisfied. "I don't follow you, Mrs. Gardner. What do you think is the trouble with the Burtons?"

She turned her head sharply to look at me, then returned her gaze to the road in front of us. "I've been around for a good many years," she said, "and it certainly doesn't take a genius to recognize typhoid fever."

I couldn't believe what I had heard. "Typhoid?" I asked stupidly. Gert trudged along steadily, obviously not caring in the least.

"I've seen it a dozen times . . . thought once I had it myself. I'm no expert," she said with a tone of voice that said the opposite, "but I'll bet anything I own that typhoid's hit that home."

I remembered when Carr had examined the couple and gave his diagnosis as either flu or food poisoning, and I found it hard to accept the enormity of his error. I said as much to Mrs. Gardner.

"Oh, I can understand a mistake early on, but not at this stage," she said. "My goodness, if he examined her, surely he saw those rosy blotches on her belly. That and the fever, and the nose bleeding, with the headaches and loose bowels and all, why I don't see how anyone could make that mistake that knows what he's about."

"He's young yet," I said. "Maybe he hasn't had much experience with typhoid." And then hopefully: "Maybe he just didn't want to upset everybody."

Lucy Gardner's laugh was more of a bark. "He is young, if that's what he believes. Only way you stop an outbreak of typhoid, far as I know, is to get everybody working together to clean the place up. You can't hide it. If it's there, it's there. Ain't no use of pretending different."

I still found the situation unlikely. "How about the medicine he sent? Even you told Paul that he should take some if he could. And Jody too."

Lucy Gardner shrugged and pulled her wrap tight. "A little whiskey will do them both good. Keeps the circulation up, gives some energy. Although, frankly, I doubt that any medicine will do Jody much good."

"You mean that?"

"She's pretty far gone. Her heart's just a flutter. And that fever, my land, I don't know how high it is, but it's too high. If she pulls through, it will be just pure luck, believe you me. She always was nothing more than a scarecrow, anyway. Almost died last year when she miscarried that baby. But," and Mrs. Gardner heaved a heavy sigh, "if it's typhoid, and I know it is, her fever will be down some in the morning. Maybe I can get some nourishment down her then."

"Is there anything else I can do?" I couldn't keep the worry out of my voice.

She sat beside me in the dark for a few seconds as we passed the first houses on the edge of Ludlum. "No," she said, "I guess I can get everything I need for the morning. Some fresh milk will ease the stomach pains, maybe find something for the headache. Mostly what it takes is rest, clean room, and prayer. You can help with the latter, if you will."

I drove Mrs. Gardner to her home on one of the back streets, along the river, and said good night. From where I sat, I could see Carr's office, but the light wasn't on. I resolved to pay him a visit first thing in the morning. I clucked the reins, and Gertrude headed us down the lane toward the stable.

CHAPTER 7

I had almost gone to sleep when a dim memory from the back of my mind jarred me to full wakefulness. I remembered the drawn, worried look on John Farraday's face the day he was killed. He had come into the office, I recalled, and then we had been interrupted by Haley, and then finally, by the accident. I searched my memory for Farraday's exact words, for now they seemed somehow important to me.

Then the pieces fell together. "I've just been upriver," Dr. Farraday had said, and he was worried. If he had been to the Burtons', and early on knew that typhoid was in that house, then he would have been concerned. As far as I could remember Ludlum had gone lucky through the years. A major epidemic had never struck town. Dr. Farraday had obviously known something none of the rest of us did.

I got up and put on my clothes hastily. With the uncertainty Mrs. Gardner had put in my mind, along with the memory of an interrupted Dr. Farraday, I had to find out for certain from Dr. Carr. I left my room at a run for the El Grande.

Avoiding the saloon for one of the few times in my life, I went straight to Belle's room. Belle Heavner ran the El Grande, and it was the best boardinghouse in Ludlum.

"Belle, what room's Dr. Carr in?" I asked as she opened her door a crack.

She eyed me suspiciously for a second or two, and her eyes twinkled. "The doctor or his sister?"

"The doc," I replied promptly, and I guess then she could see that I was in a hurry.

"Two-oh-one," she said crisply. "Any trouble?"

"No," I lied, and then decided I should leave her unconcerned. "Miss Carr is in the adjoining room?"

"I thought so," Belle said. "You vultures are all alike. Even you old ones. Yes, it's next door, but I suggest you stop by the doctor's and tell him your intentions toward his sister are entirely honorable, even at this hour."

"I'll do that," I replied, and tipped my hat to Miss Heavner, who withdrew into her room with a satisfied leer. I ran up the stairs two at a time, my mind groping for answers, and hoping that Mrs. Gardner was wrong. After several seconds, Dr. Carr answered the door. He wore a flannel nightgown but little else, despite the chill in the room.

"Yes?" He looked at me with no expression, waiting for me to state my business. I pushed past him into the room.

"Dr. Carr, I have to talk to you. It's important, otherwise I'd let it wait until morning. Do you mind if I come in?"

Carr bowed slightly and closed the door behind me. "You seem to be in," he said, with a faint trace of humor in his voice. "Of course you may see me. What's the problem?"

I came straight to the point. "Mrs. Gardner says that the Burtons have typhoid fever." Dr. Carr blinked once or twice, and his light blue eyes bored into mine.

"And?"

I was caught off guard. Obviously he knew. "Why didn't you tell Randy Kane and me earlier today, when we went out there?"

"What would have been the point of that?" Carr's cool and steady gaze didn't waver.

"Well," I said lamely, "don't you think typhoid is a little

more important than just a common cold or the influenza? Mrs. Gardner thinks Jody Burton's right on the edge."

Dr. Carr shrugged. "I'm not in the habit of discussing my patients with others, Mr. Bassett. You will sympathize, I'm sure. If a man doesn't wish to read one newspaper, he will choose another. If the Burtons are more comfortable with Mrs. Gardner as their physician"—and he stressed the word physician—"then that's their choice."

Dumbfounded by Carr's blunt attitude, I said, "But you're the one who suggested that we find them a nurse of some kind."

"Yes, I did," Carr replied. "And you have. Thank you. I know they have typhoid fever, now Mrs. Gardner knows, and you know. I hope that that's as far as it goes. But knowing women like Mrs. Gardner, I'm sure that's more than I can hope for, Mr. Bassett."

"Dr. Farraday seemed pretty upset on the day he died. I think he had just come from the Burtons' and knew it was typhoid. He said he needed help."

Carr smiled engagingly. "What can I say? I don't think the situation is all that serious." He ushered me toward the door. "But thank you for your concern. And . . ." he paused for a moment, "to keep the town from going in an uproar over nothing, you might keep this all more or less to yourself. The Burtons are some distance from town. I don't think anyone else is in any danger of contracting the disease."

I left Dr. Carr's room with mixed emotions. I'll admit that the very word typhoid scares me, but there are probably more stories about it than fact. Nonetheless, I didn't like the young physician's attitude. I was convinced that when we were out at the Burtons', he hadn't suspected typhoid as the cause of the illness.

When I returned to my room, I tried to relax by counting

the lumps in the mattress, but that didn't help. Each one reminded me of the Burton ranch.

Marc Carr leaned against the doorjamb, staring at the floor. Alice Lindsay came from her adjoining room, where she had been waiting, and her face was dark with concern.

"Do you think he's right?" she asked, and her voice was small.

Carr looked up sharply. "So what if he is? Like I said, it's an isolated case, some distance from town. It will affect nobody. Besides, the able Mrs. Gardner is out there, taking care of things."

Alice's voice was soft. "And what if it does spread?"

"We'll be long gone."

"That's all?"

"What are you saying?"

Her chin came up. "I'm saying that maybe if those two people out there had a doctor, maybe there wouldn't be that risk."

Carr laughed harshly. "I'm supposed to call a doctor? That would take some careful explaining, indeed. No, I suspect this will all blow over. We'll be busy, they're in good hands, and before much more time is up, we'll be gone."

Alice plopped down on the edge of the bed, and shook her head. "It's so foolish. Marc, we're just begging for trouble. It's a small town, everybody will know. We ought to either leave now, before they find out, or find those poor people out there a doctor." She looked at Carr, her eyes once more pleading. Carr turned and placed his hand on the door latch, opening the door to the hall gently as he looked steadily at Alice.

"Here's the door," he said softly.

Their gazes locked for several seconds in silence, and Alice was the first to break the deadlock.

"You can be awful cold sometimes," she said, and got up. Without another word, she walked quickly through the inner passage to her own room, slamming the door behind her.

Carr's lips curled slightly in a faint smile, and he gently closed the hall door. Despite the outward show of confidence, he was worried. The scheme he and Whitman had played to perfection in several larger communities across the country, always to great profit, was rapidly becoming worrisome. What he had told Alice was true, as far as he knew. Even if the Burtons were suffering from typhoid, their ranch was nearly a mile from town. Mrs. Gardner no doubt knew as much about medicine as many full-fledged physicians, anyhow. She would cover his tracks, but by the same token, she might blab his incompetence all over town.

He looked at the inner door that led to Alice's adjoining room, and frowned. Alice was the one who might panic if things didn't go right. He padded across the chilly floor and opened her door. Perhaps by morning, he thought, she would be convinced that he knew what he was doing.

I was awake before dawn that next morning, and had already worried a day's quota before the sun hit the tops of the hills behind Ludlum. What bothered me more than anything else was the recurring notion that John Farraday had known something about this incident and wanted to spread the word. I had respected Farraday's medical judgment far more than most doctors I had ever met, and at the same time, I was anything but impressed with his young replacement.

I brooded over those worries while I smoked and enjoyed one of Chase's huge cups of ever-ready coffee at the dawn-opening El Grande.

"Up kinda with the birds, ain'tcha?" Chase Hughs said as he offered me more of the strong, black coffee. Chase was a good bartender. Milt Haley told me once that Hughs had stopped more fights in that establishment single-handedly than any other man. He did it by simply closing up shop—a punishment worse than death for most of us in the valley. If there was a fight in the saloon or the small dining room of the El Grande, he closed for the remainder of the day—unless the fight happened after seven in the evening—then he closed for the whole next day. Belle backed up his policy, and so did Milt, although the marshal's help was rarely needed. It wasn't that Hughs abhorred violence . . . he could throw a punch as good as anyone else. And he kept a double-barreled shotgun loaded with a charge of nails under the bar. It was just that the glassware was so expensive, and so hard to come by, that a brawl had no place in his domain. Out on the street was fine. Then it was up to Haley or whoever else wanted to be a peacemaker.

I slid my cup over, and watched Chase fill it to the brim. "No, just couldn't sleep. Thought I might as well come over here and help you open the place—beats lying in bed and staring at the ceiling."

Chase nodded and returned the pot to the stove in a small room just off the end of the bar rail. "Haley was lookin' for you," he called, then reemerged to begin another unnecessary cleaning of the already spotless bar top.

"What'd I do?"

One side of Chase's face twitched, about the closest he ever came to a smile, let alone a laugh. He shrugged.

"When was this?" I asked.

"Yesterday," Chase said, squinting at an imaginary stain on the bar.

"Morning? Noon? Night? When? What'd he say?"

"Lemme think. Right after lunch. He was with . . ." and

the opening door interrupted him ". . . well, he kin tell you himself, then. Mornin', limpy."

Haley, bright-eyed and obviously a newsman's best friend by the look on his face, nodded at Chase and pointed at my coffee cup.

"You break your tongue, too?" Chase asked, then turned to fetch his old friend the coffee. Rumor had it that both the bartender and the marshal had grown up in the same neighborhood in Manhattan. Neither would dignify the rumor with an answer, but most of the town's "good authorities" said it was for true.

"You look a little worse for wear," Haley said to me, grinning. He had not yet shaved, and had the rumpled appearance of having slept in his clothes.

"Everyone wants to tell me that," I answered, and lit another cigarette. I tossed my bag of tobacco across, and Haley fixed himself a smoke. He lit it and took a tentative sip of the newly arrived coffee.

"I'm goin' to Bridger," he said expressionlessly.

"The knee?"

"Yep."

"So?"

"Whaddya mean, 'so.' It hurts like hell."

I laughed. "It's been hurting like hell ever since you busted it up. It's about time you decided to trust the army doctors."

"Bud Brown's goin' to fill in while I'm gone," Haley said, and he sounded doubtful. "Won't be no trouble, I don't think."

"You probably won't even be missed," I kidded. "Is that what you wanted to tell me yesterday? Chase told me."

Haley shook his head. "Nope, I got somethin' for your newspaper that ought to interest folks round about." He stopped and appeared to be examining the rim of his coffee cup.

"Well?"

"Well, so ole Whitman's dead." He looked at me, expecting a reaction, but drew a blank stare instead. Maybe it was the early morning hour, but the name didn't register.

"Whitman?" Then my mind began working again. "Oh . . . Jesus, Whitman! Doc Whitman you mean?" Haley nodded. "How? When?"

"About two days ago, they say. Over in Evanston."

"Evanston? How'd it happen?"

Haley shrugged. "From what the U.S. Marshal says, it wasn't Whitman's fault. I guess an argument broke out in a place there. Some joker's gun went off, bullet went out a window, and clipped him."

"Something about this town seems to bring bad luck to doctors," I said, still shaken by the news. "Doc Carr best mind his step."

"Yeah, but that ain't the half of it. Before he died, Whitman had a chance to say a word or two. He told one of the boys out there in Evanston that they should get ahold of his cousin, John Farraday, here in Ludlum, and let him know, and also his old ma in Cambridge, Massachusetts."

I was confused. "That don't make sense," I said.

Haley's eyebrows went up. "It don't? Just because Whitman knew Farraday was long dead? Hell's bells, of course it don't make no sense. And somethin' else that don't make sense, too, I'll tell ya. Marshal in Evanston cabled Whitman's mother all the hell and gone way back there in Massachusetts to tell her. Two bits says you don't know what happened."

"His mother was already dead, too."

Haley snorted. "Hell, no. She's alive all right, but she fired a cable right back, asking for further information."

"How come?"

"'Cause her son, Mitchell Whitman, ain't no goddamn doctor, that's why." Haley leaned back with the satisfaction of a story well told.

"Well," I groped for an answer. "Were they the same Mitchell Whitman?"

"The same." Haley leaned forward, his voice lowering. "I told you that I didn't like that little snake. Even there at the end, when he told me to go to Bridger for the knee and I kinda got to trustin' him, well, there was somethin' there all the while."

"So he was playin' doctor all along? Charged kinda high for a quack, I'll say." But there was one part of the story still confusing me, and that was Whitman's request that the law get in touch with Farraday—when he already knew him to be dead. "Why do you suppose he did that?" I asked Haley.

"Hell if I know," he answered. "But that's the only way we found out. Marshal there thought we could tell Farraday for him. I wired him back and filled him in, but he don't have no more ideas than I do. Except for them two requests, Whitman died pretty closemouthed."

I sighed. "Just goes to show that you never know. And hey, there, I got something to talk over with you," I said, having nearly forgotten the worry that resulted in my sleepless night. "We got us a problem."

"Chase! You got any more coffee?" After yelling at the bartender, Haley turned back to me. "I can't face no more problems without some more coffee."

"Well, make it strong. We got typhoid."

Haley looked at me hard and knew I wasn't joking with him. He cursed softly. "God, that's what we need right now. Who?"

"Burtons. Both of 'em."

"Bad?"

"As can be. Mrs. Gardner says Jody's like to die." The violence of Haley's palm smacking the table startled me.

"Son-of-a-bitch. And that creep Whitman was dealing with them two." His voice grew harsh. "I seen both of 'em in his office when I went to talk to him myself. Paul and him had to help Jody down the stairs. Goddamn. If he had been a real doc, maybe he could have helped some in time."

"Sure enough. And I think Farraday knew about the Burtons on the day he was killed."

Haley sat up straight, listening intently. "He came into the *Herald* office and wanted to talk to me," I continued. "We came over here, and he just about had time to tell me something was wrong 'upriver' when you came in about the Pepper boy."

"He mighta caught it in the real early-on stage, then," Haley mused.

"Yeah, but you know, it's funny. You ever know Farraday to get too shook over someone's being sick?"

"No, but we ain't had typhoid every day, neither."

"That's true. But I still think there was something on his mind. Even if he knew it was typhoid, it was several days before you saw the Burtons in town here, still able to get around. He should have been confident of catching it in time. But something tells me, if he actually was up at Burtons', that more is wrong. He said he needed my help."

"What in Christ would he need you for?" Haley's question didn't exactly come out complimentary, but I ignored that. I didn't know the answer, either.

"Well, hey," Haley said suddenly, "we still got us a doctor. What's young Carr got to say about all this?"

"Milt, there's something about this town and doctors, I swear. Randy Kane came into town to fetch help. He'd stopped by Burtons', tried to clean the place up, and knew they needed help. He didn't know Whitman had left, so I took him over to Doc Carr. Us all three went out. God, Milt, you wouldn't believe that place, how it smelled. Anyway, Doc Carr tells us that they got either the influenza, or food poisoning, or both. Nothin' about typhoid. So we come back to town, and he suggests that someone go out to Burtons' to stay awhile and help out. Says his nurse can't do it. So Mrs. Gardner goes out, with me driving. She spots it as typhoid, right off."

"So? What did Carr say?"

I told Haley about my conversation with the young doctor the night before. To my surprise, Haley agreed with Carr.

"Until we're sure, ain't no use in alarming everybody."

"People ought to know what's going on in their own town, seems to me, though," I answered. "And, besides, Carr agrees with Mrs. Gardner. So I guess we're sure."

After a pause, Haley said, "Did he think there was any risk for an epidemic?"

"No. He was real firm on that. Says they're too far from town."

"There you are, then."

One question still nagged me, though, and I repeated it again to Haley. "What was Farraday so excited about, then?"

Haley spread his hands out, palms up. "Patrick, we may never know. You don't even know he was talkin' about the Burtons. Whether he was or wasn't, don't much matter, now. Either time'll tell, or we'll never know."

CHAPTER 8

Jody Burton died Friday. After a morning respite, during which she lay in a semicoma with only a mild fever, her temperature once more began its now daily cycle, soaring higher and higher as the day progressed.

Mrs. Gardner said later that the raging temperature and unrelenting bowel hemorrhaging killed Jody. If Doc Farraday had indeed guessed the character of the disease, it meant that Jody had been fighting the typhoid for more than two weeks, and Paul Burton about the same.

Doc Farraday may or may not have been concerned, but what angered Mrs. Gardner was that Dr. Carr hadn't been. What he could've done, I don't know. And he was busy. When someone is really sick in a community, even though no one but a handful of us knew the Burtons' illness as typhoid, it seems to bring out the best and the worst. Mrs. Gardner was an example of the best but most of the rest cataloged their newly inflamed ills and trooped off to see the doctor. From my vantage point across the street, I saw the same familiar faces—a few changes, though. Mrs. Bonitis had both of her children with her this time, not just the youngest.

Alice Lindsay ushered Mrs. Bonitis into the front portion of the makeshift office. The woman was plainly distraught, and the youngest child, Kelly, was obviously more than "fretful."

Carr took the infant, a feather-light bundle, and carried

him into the rear portion of the large room, where a primitive screen shielded the examining area from the rest of the room. Alice Lindsay followed and deftly helped Carr unwrap the quilt that swathed the baby. His eyes were screwed tightly shut and his breath came in short, rapid jabs. His skin, normally so pink and full, seemed to hang in tiny folds from the undersides of his arms and even under his lower jaw, but his belly was swollen and tight, with livid pink blotches. Overall, the effect was that of a miniature ancient who had been randomly scalded with boiling water.

"Good God," Carr breathed, and looked quickly up at Alice. The girl's eyes were wet. Sensing the presence of the mother nearby, he turned. "Perhaps it would be best if you were to wait with the other child in the outer area, Mrs. Bonitis," he said, and he looked again at Alice. "We'll do what we can."

"Will he be all right?" The mother's voice was plaintive.

Carr sighed, his eyes drawn to the child before him, a child barely alive, lying on a rough, makeshift table that reminded the young man brutally of the medical care the infant needed but would never receive. "He's a very sick child. We'll do what we can."

Sensing Carr's helplessness, Alice moved quickly and ushered the woman out into the waiting area, seating her gently beside the five-year-old, who sat quietly with his legs swinging idly.

Behind the screen and working carefully, Carr took the infant's temperature, and while he waited, listened to the rapidly beating heart, its tiny butterfly pulses so thready that Carr had difficulty counting them.

With Alice once more at his side, Carr leaned heavily on the table, eyes locked on the infant's face. "Ali, I just don't know what to do," he said, voice lowered to scarcely a whisper. "It's typhoid, I know it is. It has to be. But my God, he's so . . ." and he groped for words ". . . so tiny. How can he survive a thing like this?"

He felt Alice's hand on his shoulder. "Tell her, Marc."

He spun around in sudden rage. "Tell her?" he rasped, his voice still nearly inaudible. "Tell her? And then what? What good will it do? This child is dying, Ali, and there's nothing we can do. He would never survive a stage ride to Fort Bridger, and if we say anything else, we're through. Are you ready for that?" He turned back to the infant and read the temperature. "A hundred and five." He shook his head. "We might as well leave her with some hope. There's nothing else." He ran a finger down the side of the infant's cheek, deep in thought. He moved his hand and rested it on the child's forehead, and the child responded with a feeble kick of its thin legs. "Maybe some stimulant would help keep his strength up," he said, and pointed at a row of bottles on the desk near the window.

"Are you sure?" Alice asked.

"Of course I'm not sure, Ali." He wiped his hands on his trousers. "How can I be sure? But it's all I know to do." He turned back to the infant. "With an adult, it's so easy. But with a child, my God, he's so small, and he can't tell you anything." When he looked up at Alice, his eyes were tortured. "This is never what I meant to happen." And then, straightening up, he smoothed his hair and took the bottle of elixir that Alice handed him. With firm strides, he left the room and approached Mrs. Bonitis, who immediately stood up, hands tightly clasped together.

"While Alice finishes up with Kelly, let me tell you what to do," he said, voice professionally crisp. "When he seems a little stronger, perhaps in the morning, try to get him to take a little of this. It's important right now that we keep his strength up."

"Will he be all right?" the woman repeated, as if those were the only words she could think to utter.

"He's very sick, but God willing, he'll be all right. Influenza is always so unpredictable."

"And Michael?" The woman indicated the five-year-old in the chair.

"Let's have a look at you, young man," Carr said, and as Alice handed the bundle that cradled Kelly to the anxious woman, he led the other youngster into the examining area.

Five minutes were all that were necessary to tell Carr that Michael Bonitis, while quite ill, was in no immediate danger. With the capriciousness that marked the course of typhoid, the older youngster had been spared the most vicious part of the attack. For whatever reason, his system had rebounded. His temperature was barely 102 degrees, and the characteristic rosy splotches that Carr had noticed on Jody Burton and Kelly Bonitis were nothing more than a faint rouge on Michael. Enough of what he had seen, even briefly, at the Burton ranch was present in both children's symptoms, however. Carr was now sure that Mrs. Gardner was correct, and he was also sobered by the knowledge that the typhoid had spread to the village.

Reassuring the youngster, Carr led him back to his mother.

"He'll be fine, Mrs. Bonitis. But do keep him rested. We don't want to take any chances with him doing so well."

In another two minutes, the family had left. It wasn't until much later, while examining another patient, that Carr remembered he had collected no money from Mrs. Bonitis. But the thought was as quickly dismissed from his mind.

The flow of patients during that day remained undiminished. Even Mrs. Sillitoe joined the ranks, but this time her complaint was neither imaginary nor related to her obese figure.

Dr. Carr examined her carefully, with Alice Lindsay at his side the entire time. Before he reached for the thermometer, he knew the elderly woman's problem. He listened patiently to her listless recital of the symptoms, jotted down a note or two, and then asked Alice to escort her home, where she was put to bed with strict orders to remain there. No further urging was necessary, however, for the woman, as sick as she was, could read the concern on the young man's face.

Knowing that he might have a trap building for himself that could snap shut at any moment, Carr leaned heavily back against the examining table as the two women left the office, Mrs. Sillitoe heavy on Alice's arm. Still unsure of what to do, Carr had few moments to think. Heavy footsteps sounded on the boardwalk outside, and a thick-set man pushed through the door. His watery eyes latched onto Carr's face, and his mouth split open in a rottentoothed smile.

"Hiya, Doc." And as Carr straightened up, the man stepped forward. "Think ya can fix my throat?" And he halted in mid-floor, opening his mouth so wide Carr couldn't help laughing.

"What's wrong with it?" the young man asked, and stepped up close to peer into the offered cavern. He got within a foot and recoiled. The man's breath was heavy and fetid, an unbelievable jarring symphony of rancid odors that hit Carr like a fist.

"Guess it's bad as the boys say," the man said, and wiped his lips. "They kicked me out of the bunkhouse till I see you." He paused. "Sure hurts a mite, too."

The man was so casual that Carr found it difficult to keep from convulsing with laughter at the sight of him, the ridiculousness of the situation cleaning Carr's system of worry.

"Let's rinse you out and take a good look," he said, and went into the examining area. As the man dutifully followed him, Carr selected the largest bottle of alcohol he could find and poured a liberal glassful. Handing it to the man, he indicated the back door. "Take this, all of it, and rinse out your mouth. Wouldn't hurt to gargle, if you can. Then we'll see."

The man grabbed the glass in grubby fingers and did as he was told, a performance of loud gagging, spitting, and sniffing. Finally he returned, tears in his eyes.

"Now let's have a look," Carr said, and this time the alcohol almost masked the other odors. The man's throat was livid red and swollen, and even the inside of his mouth was mildly inflamed. "Well, now, Mr. . . ."

"Harry Curran," the man said, and closed his mouth.

"Well, Mr. Curran, I can see that your throat would hurt some. It's red as a sunset."

"Boys say it's the Cat's Claw."

"The what?"

"Cat's Claw," Curran repeated, and dug in his back pocket. He handed Carr a rumpled packet of chewing tobacco, and the young man took it and unfolded it. He looked at the coarse mixture, more stems than anything else, and then at Curran. The man grinned. "Boys say it's more barn sweepin's than tobacco, but I like 'er."

Carr handed the pouch back. "You chew a lot of that?"

"Alla time," Curran said, nodding. "Boys say I shouldn't swaller it."

"Do what?"

"I swaller it," the man said, as if explaining to a child. "Can't spit. Ain't got enough teeth, I guess. Always ends up on my chin, most of it. Besides, I like the taste."

Carr laughed. "How long you been on that stuff, Mr. Curran?"

The man shrugged. "Oh, I get it cheap, see. I get a good deal on it. I guess I been chewing since I could walk, one way or another."

Folding his arms, Carr sat on the edge of the table. "The way I see it, Mr. Curran, is that your throat's just agreeing with the boys. It's about had enough Cat's Claw. That's pretty strong stuff to choke down day in, day out. Your throat's all inflamed, and I bet you a ten-dollar piece that the tobacco's the blame."

"What you think I oughtta do, Doc?"

Carr shrugged. "Give it up for a while."

Curran's forehead furrowed in thought. It was obvious the suggestion didn't sit well with him. He looked at Carr. "Give up chewin'?"

"Or take up spitting, one or the other. Your throat can't take much more. First thing you know, you won't be able to breathe at all."

"Gol dang," the rancher said, and shook his head. "If ya can't chew, now just what can a man do?" He looked helpless.

Carr laughed and slapped the man on one beefy shoulder. "It'll get better after a while, then you can go back. But you ought to cut down some, if you can, or you'll be right back the same way. Try chewing on sticks."

"Sticks?"

"Yeah. I used to do that when I was a kid. Always had a twig in my mouth. But let me give you something to make that throat feel a little better." Carr rummaged through his large valise and found a small bottle of Dr. Clausen's, a mixture that was mostly honey. Curran accepted the bottle, squinted at the label, and gave up.

"Looks all dried up," he said.

"Yes, crystal form," Carr said quickly. "Just heat the bottle in hot water for a few moments, and it turns liquid. Take as much as you need."

Curran nodded in appreciation of the wonders of modern medicine and thrust the bottle into his pocket. With a burst

of energy that startled Carr, the rancher stuck out his hand
and shook Carr's vigorously.

"Thanks, Doc. Boys said you could help. Much obliged."

"Any time," Carr said.

"How much I owe ya?"

Shrugging, Carr smiled. "Let's say five dollars now, and if
you need to come back, well it's on the house. That's the
best guarantee I can give."

Curran paid willingly and left, the Cat's Claw in one
pocket of his baggy trousers, the Dr. Clausen's in the other.
Watching his retreating figure, Carr laughed quietly. "Now
that's one that wasn't on Mitchell's list," he said out loud,
and nudged the door closed with his foot. The money in his
pocket was a comfortable weight.

It wasn't until much later in the afternoon that I saw Mrs.
Gardner being driven past in a wagon by Randy Kane. Her
face was grim, and I could see the covered body in the back
of the buckboard. They didn't stop but drove straight
through town to the funeral parlor.

I assumed immediately, and as it turned out, correctly,
that it was Jody Burton who silently occupied the back of
the buckboard, under the tarpaulin. But Jody wasn't alone
under the cover—she had company. Kane had stopped by to
talk to Cyril Garcia. What with his worrying about the Burtons and his own chores, he hadn't seen Garcia since the
neighbors had taken sick. Garcia was a loner anyway, and
no one seemed just sure how he did earn a living. But no
one needed to worry about that now. Garcia had been found
dead, and it was obvious from his condition and the smell
and mess in his small shack that he had lost a vicious bout
with the typhoid.

Mrs. Gardner didn't waste any time at the funeral parlor.
Not a half hour later, she was driven back through town by

the obedient Kane, who had given himself the job as official caretaker for the Burtons—now Paul Burton alone, lying racked with fever, bleeding and running from both ends. Mrs. Gardner didn't stop at Doc Carr's office, and that frankly surprised me.

Seeing her pass his office, I got up and walked out into the street, intercepting the buckboard. Kane stopped, and Mrs. Gardner, in a voice clipped with anger and frustration and weakened with fatigue, told me about Jody and Cyril.

"Are you going to talk to Dr. Carr?" I asked, because that was the thing that worried me the most—the young doctor's almost flippant attitude. She looked down at me as if I was a five-year-old trying her patience.

"Mr. Bassett," she said, "*Dr.* Carr"—and she leaned on the word "Doctor" as if it were an insult—"didn't examine Jody Burton closely enough to tell what her problem was. I can forgive that. I don't understand it, with typhoid being as easy to recognize as the devil himself, but I can forgive it. But now that he knows what the problem is, he seems bound to ignore it. That I can't forgive."

"Does he know about Garcia?"

"How can he? He hasn't stuck his head out of that office. He's jabbering with every hypochondriac that this town has to offer and making a handsome dollar at it, too, I'll wager."

I frowned. "I tried to talk with him about it, but he as much as told me, pardon me, ma'am, to go to hell."

Mrs. Gardner laughed shortly. "And that's exactly what is likely to happen, if it hasn't started already."

"What do you mean?"

"I mean, Mr. Bassett, that you could well spend your time, if you have nothing pressing, warning every soul you can reach in this town. Mr. Kane here has told me some distressing news. The linen," and she paused dramatically, "was washed out in the creek."

"And?" I felt that I should know what was coming, but I confess I didn't know what the elderly woman was driving at.

"Typhoid fever is frequently passed by unsanitary conditions, and frequently by water. Now some folks in this village drink water from Ghost Creek, especially when the wells get low. Mr. Kane here," and she nodded once more at the uncomfortable Randy, "says that he couldn't face washing the linen of the Burtons' in the tub, so he took them down to the creek. I wouldn't doubt that Paul Burton did the same thing before he became too ill to move. It wouldn't surprise me if contagion in the water laid Mr. Garcia low, and he may have washed himself off in the creek too, it being so much easier than a tight tub when you're ailing." She stopped and resituated herself on the buckboard seat. "So, Mr. Bassett, what I'm predicting is that we're going to see typhoid in this village, and soon. Anyone who has drunk out of that stream, and they may be legion, especially children, and maybe anyone who has gone swimming in that water hole behind the church . . . and those are legion, and those"—she paused and sighed heavily—"are also children."

I looked unconsciously at my hands, remembering how I had helped with some of that linen. "Christ," I said, and gazed off toward the creek, just behind the buildings.

"I'll talk with your Dr. Carr this evening, after I'm sure that Paul will pass the day's crisis. He is stronger than his wife, and I am optimistic, God willing. And perhaps it would be wiser after all if you were to wait before alerting everyone, until after we've talked with the young man. After all, he is a physician."

The pieces were all together in my mind now. If Doc Farraday had learned from Paul Burton—maybe even from Jody herself—that early on the soiled linen had been washed in the creek, then he would have come to the same conclusion as Mrs. Gardner. I doubted that her experience was leading her far astray. The only trouble was Doc Farraday had probably discovered the truth weeks earlier, when it was just budding. Now, he was dead . . . and so were two others.

Cagey as she was, Mrs. Gardner was wrong about one thing. Dr. Carr had seen her and Randy Kane drive by in the buckboard, and by the set of their faces and the cover over the back of the wagon, he right away knew the cargo. But his concern was triggered by more than the slow-moving buckboard and what it meant. Danger tends to make anyone but a fool more alert, and Carr was no fool. He had learned enough basic medicine in college—even though his training was a scant two years—to put up a good front, and he knew enough medicine to recognize the obvious.

As he watched the wagon pass, he leaned on the sill, thinking hard. That afternoon, he had examined the Bonitis boys. And the aging Mrs. Sillitoe. From what he had seen at the Burtons', and from what Mrs. Gardner had said, he was sure that typhoid was in the village.

True enough, he had sent them all home to bed with an ample supply of elixirs. Some of the alcohol might even do some good. But Marc Carr knew that he was trapped, and as he watched the buckboard rumble out of sight, his hands were clammy. If that wagon did indeed hold Jody Burton's remains, there would be questions, and Carr knew he would not be able to answer them.

Curran had left the office, Alice had returned, and two more patients had left their money. One was quickly treated for a badly sprained wrist, and the other for what Carr suspected was nothing more than a simple earache. After they left, Carr closed the door and bolted it. It was late in the afternoon, and he pulled the curtains across the window to cut off the glare of the lowering sun.

"Alice?" he called, and the girl came out of the examining area where she had been freshening up. She was still tying up her hair, and for a moment Carr stood still and enjoyed the sight of the girl in the white dress.

"What is it, Marc?"

"We're leaving. Tonight."

Alice Lindsay stopped where she was and her face mirrored the worry Carr felt. "What happened." And it was not a question, but a statement coming after a long period of expectation—one that had built for several days.

"Nothing," Carr lied badly. "It's just time, that's all."

"It's the typhoid, isn't it?" she asked, and she moved close and laid a hand on Carr's sleeve. "Isn't it?" she repeated softly at his silence. Seeing the misery on his face, Alice was frightened by what had so suddenly caught them up.

When he spoke, his voice was husky. "I just saw that old lady and the guy from up-creek go by in the buckboard. It had a body in the back, covered up. It must have been that woman at the ranch. Mrs. Gardner's been up there, and that's all it could be." Alice said nothing, and Carr continued. "Old ladies like Mrs. Gardner are smart enough. I'm sure now that she called it right."

"You knew that before," Alice said quietly.

"Yeah," Carr laughed humorlessly. "But now it's in town. You saw them as well as I. The two children, old lady Sillitoe. I don't know how it traveled so fast, but it's here, in town."

"It couldn't be anything else? Couldn't it be a coincidence?"

"You know it's nothing else. You saw those two boys."

"What are you going to do?"

"Like I said, it's time for us to leave. There's nothing we can do here."

"Shouldn't we tell someone?" Alice insisted.

Carr laughed again, abruptly, at his fiancée's innocence. "They know already. Believe me, they know. If we stay, they'll have us right in the middle of it. We can't let that happen. Maybe the best thing is to clear out now, and that'll force them to find someone else—maybe down at Bridger. There's at least two doctors there, I've heard. It'll be best all around. We won't get caught, and they'll have themselves a doctor that's a doctor."

"I feel sorry for them," Alice said quietly.

Carr shrugged. "It happens. The best thing we can do is leave. Tonight. I'll find a wagon that no one'll miss right away, and we can be at the railhead in a day or two, in time to catch a train west to Evanston. We can meet Whitman . . ." He was interrupted by the door opening, and the name of his partner died hanging in mid-air as Milt Haley stepped in. Carr looked nonplussed for only a fraction of a second, then swiftly regained his composure. He smiled broadly and greeted Haley, his stomach all the while a tight knot of nerves. Haley gave no sign of having overheard the conversation between Carr and the girl.

"Hiya, Doc, and Miss." He tipped his hat at Alice Lindsay. "Kinda nasty thing about Miz Burton and old Garcia."

"Garcia?"

Haley nodded vigorously. "Did you know he was sick? Course you wouldn't have," he continued, "since you never met the man. Yeah, I guess the typhoid got him too. He was a neighbor down this way some from Paul's place."

"I'm sorry to hear that," Carr said. "I wish I'd known." Carr was not surprised that Haley knew about the typhoid, but he was uneasy nevertheless.

"No way you could've," Haley replied. "Just hope it don't

run down the valley." He looked appraisingly at Carr. "But that's not why I stopped by. I'd just guess that it's all clear for you to use old Doc Farraday's office now, if you've a mind to. Might be some medicines there you could use about now."

Carr raised his eyebrows. "Oh?" he said and waited for Haley to continue. The marshal shifted his weight and leaned against the doorjamb.

"Yep. I picked up an interesting bit of news, and I thought, well, now, maybe this'll clear things. Remember that guy who was doctorin' here just before you came, and suddenly lit out?"

Carr's stomach turned another knot, but his face remained impassive. Alice had discreetly retreated back into that portion of the large room reserved for examinations, and Carr was glad of that.

"You mean Dr. Whitman?"

"He's the one," Haley said. "He got himself killed over in Evanston."

This time, Carr was unsuccessful in keeping expression from his face. "What!" he cried loudly, the astonishment seeming only natural to Haley.

"Yep," the marshal continued. "Just an accident, but he's dead nonetheless. Weren't no doctor, neither."

Carr heard the last words only faintly through his panic, but they registered. "What do you mean?"

"Just that. Found out he weren't no doctor. Just before he died, he told the boys over there to let Doc Farraday know, here in Ludlum. Now, that's odd, 'cause he knew as well as anyone that Farraday was already dead. He also told 'em to let his old ma somewheres back East know, too, and she's the one that told 'em that her son wasn't no doctor. All seems pretty strange to me."

"Indeed," Carr managed.

"But," Haley continued, his voice pleasant, "at least he won't be pulling the wool over no one else's eyes. Jody Burton might be alive today if that quack hadn't been what he was." He moved toward the door. "Anyhow, I didn't want to take all your time jawing, but I thought you might like to know. Thought maybe you'd like to reconsider about that office."

"Thank you for stopping by," Carr replied. "I'll think on it." And he closed the door behind Haley as the marshal left.

Alice came into the main room, her face pale. "Do you think he knew?"

Carr turned on her angrily. "Keep your voice down," he rasped, then added, "Of course he didn't. Otherwise he would have said so. It's just as he says, he thought we'd like to know, since we took over after he left. It's natural. Poor Mitch, though," he said heavily. "What a thing to have happen, after all this time."

"I wonder what did happen. I didn't hear Mr. Haley say."

"He didn't. But we can thank Mitch that he had the presence of mind to send us a message, in his own way. He always was smart, that guy. He must have known that in a town this small, we'd hear about a message sent for Farraday. And one thing's for sure. The way the marshal talked, he's pinning that woman's death on Mitch, and that means on us, if he ever finds out." He squeezed Alice's shoulders. "Tonight's the night, Ali. All the way to San Francisco, without any more stops. The game's over."

Alice sighed deeply. "I just hope so, Marc. It's no fun anymore," and she almost managed a smile at her own understatement. "It's turned into an ugly mistake, and I don't mind telling you that I'm scared sick."

Carr kissed her gently on the forehead. "I know. So am I. But there's nothing either of us can do here. No one knows about us yet, and we're safe. We can leave tonight. No one will ever know where we went."

"But they'll know what we were," she said, and her eyes were filled with tears.

"Maybe not even that," Carr said, but he knew that he was wrong. He could sense it. Whitman had been correct when he said Haley was smart. Tomorrow, when they were reported gone, Haley would start putting pieces together. Carr shivered, already feeling like a man hunted. And Jody Burton had given Ludlum the quarry.

CHAPTER 9

A meadowlark sang its fool head off that evening, oblivious, like nearly everyone else in town, to the mantle of ill fortune that was wrapping itself tighter and tighter around Ludlum.

Word travels quickly, and Mrs. Gardner was in a dither. She had come back from the Burton ranch for a much needed rest but still took the time to visit with Mrs. Buchanan, a practice she had followed for years. It was from the older woman that she found out about Mrs. Sillitoe, and a half hour later, after another brief visit, she knew that her obese friend had typhoid fever. Ten minutes after that, she knew too about the Bonitis children, and at that point she decided to pay her promised visit to Dr. Carr.

She could not find the young physician. The office was locked with curtains drawn and no one answered her knock. Late in the evening though it was, running on raw nerves and nearly at the point of exhaustion herself, Mrs. Gardner nonetheless resolutely stumped over to the El Grande, stopping at the bottom of the stairs to regain her breath and let the dizziness of fatigue settle out. She caught Chase's eye, and when the bartender came over, she took a deep breath and said, "Is the young doctor in?" Chase shrugged.

"Don't know, ma'am. I ain't seen him, but that don't mean nothin'. Belle's stepped out, so she ain't around. You want me to run up to two-oh-one and see?"

Mrs. Gardner was so intent on confronting Carr immedi-

ately that she shook her head at Chase's logical offer. "No,"
she said, catching her breath again. "I'll just go on up." She
nodded at Chase and set her mind at toiling up the steep
stairway that filled the room between the saloon on the left
and the rooming house on the right. At the top, she again
paused to catch her breath, and looked down the narrow
hall for Carr's room. She walked to 201 and rapped on the
door, breathing heavily still. With no response, she rapped
again, and this time called, "Dr. Carr? It's Lucy Gardner."
Again with no answer, she tried the door, and found it
unlocked. She swung the door just far enough to see that the
room was empty, with no clothes, no personal effects, nothing to indicate that anyone was in occupancy.

Feeling uneasy, Mrs. Gardner closed the door and stood
in the hall for a moment, the dim light fading in through the
hall window making her appear small and pale. At last, she
straightened, sighing deeply, and turned toward the stairs
again. She resolved to check the office of the doctor more
carefully, and then she would go to Milton Haley. He would
certainly know where the doctor was.

Milt Haley did not know where Carr was. Neither did I.
Haley and I were enjoying a quiet before-bedtime nightcap
in his office. In all truth, it was actually about our fourth
nightcap, but we were not keeping accurate count.

"You sure he's not in his apartment?" Haley asked, in response to Mrs. Gardner's brief query about Carr's where-
bouts.

"The apartment is empty," she replied.

Haley looked over the top of the glass at me. "Empty?
You mean he's moved out of the El Grande?"

Mrs. Gardner shrugged slightly. "None of his effects are
in his room."

"Did you check the room where his sister is staying?" I
asked helpfully.

Mrs. Gardner's eyebrows shot up. "I didn't think of that. And I would think she would have heard me out in the hall in any case."

Haley set his glass down and stood up, still obviously favoring his left knee. "Well, since you're looking for him this time of day, it must be important, so let's find him. Patrick, as long as you ain't got nothin' to do, swing back over to the El Grande for me, and double-check both rooms. Twist Chase's arm, or Belle's, if she's there. I'll go on over to the doc's office and make sure he ain't off in the back somewhere with some . . ." he hesitated and shot a glance at Lucy Gardner, ". . . friend."

As I got up to join the exodus, Mrs. Gardner asked, "And if he is in neither place?"

Haley was taken aback. "Well, Mrs. Gardner, if he ain't to home, what is it you propose I do? He is free to come and go, after all. There's a million and one places he could be. Maybe with any one of hundreds of folks spread up and down this valley. If he ain't about, then whatever urgent business you have with him will just have to wait until he shows, probably in the morning."

"Marshal," Mrs. Gardner said, and her voice was like steel, "as near as I can make out, there are probably a half dozen people in this town," and she leaned heavily on those last three words, "who more than likely have typhoid fever. And it's becoming clearer and clearer that Dr. Carr is refusing to treat the illness for what it is. I simply must talk with him before the situation is completely out of control."

"Who are you talking about that's sick?" Haley asked, and there was some alarm in his voice.

"Both Bonitis children . . . Mrs. Sillitoe. And if the children have it, then it's a fair bet that some other youngsters with whom they play may also be in grave danger. Their families as well."

"Let's go, Patrick," Haley said, opening the door into the dark street.

Mrs. Gardner had been right. Carr was not in his apartment. After a quick check, it was immediately obvious that Carr and his sister were no longer residents of the hotel. Chase knew nothing about the pair, and Belle was gone. I quickly crossed the street, noticing that no light shone in Farraday's second-floor office, and walked down the boardwalk to the room Carr had taken in Woodstock's. I felt relief when I saw a light in the window. The door stood open, and I entered, expecting to find the doctor in heated conversation with Haley and Mrs. Gardner, but my hopes soon were dashed. Haley was standing in the center of the room, his hands on his hips, and when he saw me, he shook his head.

"Ain't a soul here," he muttered. "Everythin's gone. Looks like he cleaned the place out."

"Never was much here in the way of office stuff," I said hopefully.

"Well, there ain't nothin' here now," the marshal replied. "I don't know what the hell to tell you, ma'am. Sure looks mighty odd. Maybe he found a more likely place to set up shop, somewheres else in town. Seems to me a damn odd time of day to be movin' your place of business about."

The three of us went back out into the street, with Haley carefully closing the door behind us. "Lemme go around and ask old Woodstock if the doc moved out. He'd know, seeing as how he was renting the place." Mrs. Gardner and I waited on the boardwalk in silence, and in five minutes, Haley returned. "He don't know any more'n we do," he said, discouraged. Silently he rolled and then lighted a cigarette. It must have been the somewhat comical look of the three of us standing in the dark under the wooden cover of the boardwalk that caused Will Cavenaugh to laugh as he

walked past, obviously headed across the street toward the
El Grande from the stable where he left his horse while in
town.

"Evenin' gents, and you, Miz Gardner," he said, and
tipped his rumpled hat. "You all lose somethin'?"

"Lookin' to find us one misplaced doc," Haley replied
without humor.

The big lumberman stopped and stepped up on the walk.
"How's that?"

"You ain't seen Doc Carr, have you?" When the marshal
asked that question, I was expecting just another blank look,
but such was not the case.

"You mean that young squirt? The one with the purty gal
hitched up as a nurse? I ain't never really met him, you
know. Just seen him about a couple times. Ain't had no bad
hurts up the hill since he come to town. But, yep, I seen
him, least I guess it was him and his gal."

"That's his sister," Mrs. Gardner said stiffly, always a
guardian of propriety.

"When did you see him?" Haley prompted impatiently. I
could see we were fortunate to have caught Cavenaugh before he started his night's drinking.

"No more'n two hours ago. Least, as I say, I thought it
was him. Drivin' a wagon down there along the river road.
Was kinda dark, though. I was comin' up after tryin' to pry
Ben Pepper loose for the evenin'."

"The river road?" I asked, puzzled. "I wonder where he
was headed. Not too many folks live down that way."

Cavenaugh laughed good-naturedly. "You oughtta ask
folks where they's goin' before you loan 'em your wagon,
pal. Ain't yours the one with the one hind wheel that never
got black on it?"

"My wagon?"

"Hell, yes. Couldn't miss it. Think I could forget you gettin' all ouchy when you busted that back wheel up by my
mill? Well, this young fella's got your wagon, bigger'n life.
Course, I didn't think anything of it, 'cause I figured you
knew. I mean"—and his eyes twinkled—"ain't every day a
man loses a wagon right out from under his nose."

"My stars," Mrs. Gardner said helplessly.

I turned to Haley, feeling stupid. "He's got my wagon."

"Looks like," Haley snorted, and turned toward his office.
"'Spect I ought to ask him why. They shouldn't be hard to
catch up with. That road splits just past the trail up to
Peppers', and it ought to be easy to pick up fresh wagon
tracks whichever way they went. Will, thanks for the information." He turned to Mrs. Gardner. "Ma'am, I don't know
what to tell you, except you might as well be patient until I
get back with some answers. Maybe the doc's got a pretty
good explanation for what he's up to. Meantime, if there's
anything you can do for thems that's sick, why, you go on
right ahead. Patrick, I'd invite you to come along, but I
doubt there's to be any trouble. Besides, the way you ride a
horse, we'd never catch up with 'em." He grinned shortly at
me. "I'll get you back your wagon. And maybe someday, I'll
even get me time to get this knee fixed."

Through all of this, Cavenaugh stood with his mouth
slack. "What's goin' on, anyways?" he asked finally, watching Haley limp quickly off into the night.

"I don't know yet, Will," I answered, deliberately avoiding any mention of the typhoid that was settling in on the
village.

Cavenaugh shook his head in confusion. "That young
doc's actin' kinda funny, then, ain't he?"

Mrs. Gardner merely harrumphed, so I answered instead.
"Indeed he is, Will, indeed he is."

Ten o'clock had come and gone when Mrs. Gardner parted company with me and walked away in the direction of the Bonitis home, a small but well-constructed frame house half a block behind Woodstock's, perched near the tumble of rocks that kept the river from wandering into Main Street. "I'll attend to the youngest first," she said, and I knew that more than one task lay ahead—Mrs. Bonitis, with her drover husband Frank away on a cattle run, had no idea what disease in all likelihood lurked in her home.

Not knowing what else to do, I walked over to the El Grande. Thinking always makes me thirsty, and confusion doubles the thirst. Only a matter of hours had passed since a handful of people had found out that the fever was passing into the village, and it would be only a matter of hours before everyone else must know as well. Perhaps we had hesitated too long already, but looking back now, I realize we were waiting, even Mrs. Gardner, for some word of direction from Marc Carr. As natural as it may have seemed at the time to resolve the reason for the doctor's sudden departure, it stayed our hand. And I guess we paid for that mistake in the days to come.

Word of the telegram about Whitman had spread through town, naturally enough. The telegraph operator was a good one, but he could be blabby when no absolute confidence seemed called for. Through one tendril of the vine or another, nearly everyone in the area knew that Whitman had been a fraud. There was incredulity, and resentment, and embarrassment at being taken so easily. Carr's absence added to all that in my mind. As I sat in the El Grande, ignoring everyone else, none of the traditional roads open to a journalist seemed open to me. There was no one to blame— that always makes a good headline—and I hesitated in sounding an alarm. Haley had suggested waiting until we knew where we stood, and I took that as sound advice. I couldn't even write about the theft of a wagon, if that is what it was, until Haley returned.

"You want another one?" Chase's quiet voice interrupted my thoughts, and I looked up somewhat absently.

"Yes, I do," I said, and Chase nodded and took my empty mug, returning a moment later with a refill.

"Where'd gimpy head off to?" he asked, wiping his hands. The question took me by surprise, and obviously it showed. "Saw him ride out all in a hurry," Chase explained, nodding toward the front window, then he jerked his head over toward the back of the room, where Will Cavenaugh was playing solitaire, a large stein of beer at his elbow. "Besides, Will there said something about the doc borrowing your wagon without your say-so."

I took a deep breath and a bigger mouthful from the mug, then replaced the mug carefully on the table. "Yeah, Milt's just going out to check," I said, then skirted the truth a little, "to see if the doc needs any help with anything." Chase's eyebrows went up a little, but he just said, "Oh," and went back behind the bar. I shot another glance over at Cavenaugh, but he seemed engrossed in his card game and probably hadn't even seen me come in. There were only three people in the room at that moment, but the atmosphere seemed to hang heavily, and my imagination told me that everyone was doing just what I was doing—waiting.

CHAPTER 10

Where the river road forks, the paths are deep with river-bank sand. The main trail continues on south, eventually finding its way down to the Union Pacific railhead and Fort Bridger. The other fork soon peters out into little more than rock scratches in some spots, but if you work at it, it heads nearly due west for perhaps forty miles. It's used by miners, trappers, and lumbermen. Will Cavenaugh is the only man I've ever known who regularly and cheerfully runs lumber over that trail. After a bit, that trail again forks, one running north toward the headwater country of Bear River, the other trail working down through the hills toward the main route to Salt Lake.

When Haley reached the River Road fork, he dismounted and tried to make sense of the jumble of tracks in the sand. The moon was a faint and unhelpful crescent. Exasperated, the marshal turned up the wick of his small lantern until the black smoke billowed. The most promising pair of tracks, still uncut by others, made it a good bet Carr and the girl had headed south. Haley paused a moment, deep in thought. "Yeah," he muttered to himself, "they wouldn't strike out cross-country."

He swung carefully onto his horse making sure the lantern was completely snuffed, and he slung its hoop handle over the saddle horn so that it hung nearly upright against the saddle leather.

Haley knew the south fork well, and indeed for the first

two miles, the path was reassuringly wide and marked with deep soft ruts. Shortly after beginning a rise into the bluffs beside the river, however, the trail dwindled, and Haley knew anyone unfamiliar with the trail, especially in a wagon, was in for a rough and jouncing ride. For perhaps an hour he rode silently and slowly, and on occasion he caught the shadow of a fresh wagon rut where there were fewer stones.

It was nearly midnight when he halted the horse, slid carefully down, favoring his left leg, and pulled out his pocket watch, holding its face only inches from his eyes until the shadow of its hands gave away their position. He was sliding it back into his pocket when he heard a voice carried to him on the night air, thin and evanescent, yet leaving him with no doubt that he had heard a human talking. He froze, listening, but heard nothing for many minutes, until the horse nicker came through the woods clear and loud. Instinctively, he put his hand on the muzzle of his own animal, and he knew that the horse he was hearing had picked up his scent, wafted ahead by the not quite still air. To have heard the voices against even a faint stir of air told Haley that he was close, and he stroked his horse's face quietly in the dark as he planned his approach. The sounds had come from a shallow ravine in front of him, perhaps two hundred yards away. The spot would be a good place to camp, with hills sheltering both sides from view.

Moving as carefully as he could, he looped the reins of his horse around the trunk of a Gambel oak beside the trail, then removed the well-worn Winchester from the saddle scabbard. He was confident that he would have no need of the gun, and habit more than anything else prompted him as he silently drew the lever down until the bolt began its back stroke. In the dark he slid the little finger of his left hand into the space left by the bolt, and felt the brass cartridge half in and half out of the chamber. Satisfied, he closed the lever, hearing the faint chuck as the bolt once again pushed the cartridge fully home. Making sure the hammer was on safety, he swung the rifle under his arm and walked down the path.

For perhaps ten minutes he silently limped along the trail, taking his time not to trip over rocks that jutted from the soil. So dark was the ravine that he might well have walked right through the camp had it not been for the faint smell of the dead embers, so out of place in the mingle of living odors passed to him from the woods. He stopped immediately, eyes searching the dark, and the nicker of the horse seemed to leap at him, so close he inadvertently startled. He sensed more than saw movement to his left, and knew it was the horse. He had still to take another step when he heard a voice, this time to his right, and no more than thirty feet away. Even though he did not understand the words, he knew it was the girl, and he smiled grimly as he heard Carr's voice, husky and low, reassuring the girl. "She's just talking to herself," he heard Carr say, and Haley, standing in the dark, remembered that the horse taken along with the wagon was a mare.

Again the girl spoke, too faintly for Haley to understand, and this time there was exasperation in Carr's voice when he answered. "No," Carr said, none too softly this time. "Nobody is going to be following us, especially at night. If you don't settle down, neither one of us is going to get any sleep." There was silence for a long moment, and Haley was unsure of his next move. He could easily follow the trail back to town in the dark by himself, but he had no desire to keep track of two other people and a wagon while he picked out the path. The other option was one that appealed to him, since it involved doing nothing but remaining quiet. He backed up carefully until his hands touched a large pon-

derosa pine, and using that as a guide, he slowly, an inch at
a time, sank down so that he was sitting at the base of the
tree, facing the camp. Figuring that it was close to one
o'clock, he resigned himself to several hours without a
smoke. Otherwise he was satisfied. He knew where his
quarry was.

Occasionally he heard movement from the two bedrolls
thirty feet away, and he took a grim satisfaction knowing
that the couple were probably spending a night as sleepless
as his.

The girl's voice startled him into attention again.

"Are you sure that this is the trail that Mitch took?" Carr
didn't answer immediately, but Haley could hear him turning over in his bedroll.

"Why do you ask that?" Carr asked.

The girl's voice sounded both tired and forlorn. "Because
I want to feel sure that it will lead us somewhere, and not
just out into the middle of the mountains."

"Don't be silly."

"I'm not silly. How do you know this is the right road?"

"Because," Carr said, his voice heavy with patience, "we
came in on this trail on the stage. There is no other. Lots of
people do. Even the big lumber wagons use it."

The girl didn't sound satisfied. "But it's so rough."

"That's because it's dark. We won't need to travel after
dark again, now that we're away from the village." Carr
sighed loudly. "Are we going to lay here awake all night?"

"Probably," the girl replied, and Haley, thirty feet away,
grinned maliciously. "It's not comfortable and besides, I'm
scared."

"There's not much I can do to help that, Ali. We got in a
bind, and we got out of it. We're safe now, that's all I can
say. We're on our way to San Francisco."

"What are we going to do about Mitch?" Again Haley heard the name.

"You've asked that before," Carr snapped. "Just what the hell am I supposed to do? He's dead, and that's all there is to it."

"I still think you should write something to his mother. After that telegram that the marshal told us about, she must think it was someone else. She deserves to know that it was her son."

"I'll write and explain everything when we're in San Francisco," Carr said, little knowing that a man sat a pebble's throw away who was wrestling with a decision now more urgent than before.

The random pieces made sense now. If these two, with a stolen wagon and horse, were running from something in the middle of the night and were obviously concerned with the posthumous welfare of one fake doctor, then it became obvious to Haley that Carr was not what he had seemed. Mrs. Gardner's obvious displeasure with the young man echoed in Haley's mind, and the answer was reinforced. Of course Carr hadn't done what Mrs. Gardner had thought he should do—he wasn't a physician. Just how the scheme worked Haley was not sure, but he was sure, feeling the rough bark of the ponderosa on his back, that the man and woman tossing and turning a mere thirty feet away in the dark were not doctor and nurse.

"They'll lynch 'em," Haley said to himself, thinking of what the village's reaction would be when they knew the truth. Trying to frame the edges of the puzzle kept him busy until the darkness on the surrounding hilltops began to soften.

For more than two hours he had heard nothing from the couple in the camp. Either they whispered so quietly he didn't hear, or they had finally found a few moments of rest.

As he watched the sky begin to accent the bluffs, Haley
stretched and yawned, getting the kinks out of weary mus-
cles. He resented having to sit out in the woods all night
with a sore knee, resented having to limp down the rough
trail, trying to walk and remain quiet at the same time. He
resented not being able to smoke, but as the sky lightened,
he gave in.

"If it wakes 'em up, then it just wakes 'em up," he
thought. "It's time to move on anyway." For a moment he
toyed with the idea of firing off a volley from the Winchester, imagining with pleasure what the shattering report
would do to the nerves of the sleepers a few feet away. He
let the thought die, and carefully rolled a fat cigarette in the
dark. Finished, he stuck it in the corner of his mouth and
groped for a match. He cupped the flame in his hand, keeping his eyes closed so the sudden flare wouldn't ruin his
night vision, shook the match out and drew deeply. It was
light enough that he could see the smoke faintly wafting up
into the limbs above him as the morning air began to slip up
the canyon.

He was gratified two minutes later when he saw the faint
hump of the bedrolls stir, and he could dimly make out a
figure now sitting up. "Time to put the coffee on," he said,
and in the quiet predawn air, his voice was as effective as a
rifle shot. The girl let out a strangled screech. She had been
sitting up not because she sensed anything wrong but because a pebble under her bedroll had finally won its battle.
She heard his voice but didn't see him, despite his proxim-
ity. Instead she grabbed at Carr, hauling him nearly upright
and awake at the same time.

"What the hell is going on?" Carr asked groggily, but
Alice was too frightened to utter an explanation of her be-
havior.

Haley stood up stiffly, putting his weight on his good leg,

and hefted the Winchester so that he held it in the crook of his arm. "I said it was about time to put the coffee on," he repeated, and walked stiffly up to where the couple were sitting. Carr recognized him in the dim light, and swore under his breath.

"I think it best that any move you make be real slow," Haley said, but the warning was needless.

Carr spoke quickly, "I don't have a gun. You don't need the rifle." He was now alert, and Haley could see, even in the poor light, the confidence on the young man's face. Haley took another step closer, and held the muzzle of the .44 caliber rifle two inches from the man's face. He heard the girl gasp and saw her shrink back.

"Let's make one thing real straight, pal," Haley said harshly, "you may not have a gun, as you say." He shoved the rifle so that the barrel touched Carr's forehead. "But you do not tell me what I do or do not need." As he saw the self-assuredness drain from the face, he removed the rifle and slung it back over his arm. "It's time we was headin' back to town. Man there wants his wagon and horse back."

"Can we give you back the horse and wagon here, and you let us go on?" Carr asked, and he somehow made the request sound reasonable.

Haley laughed shortly. "If that'd been the case, I sure as hell wouldn't have sat here all night to wait for a fool wagon."

Alice Lindsay's hands flew up to cover her mouth, and Carr looked nervously past Haley. "Where were you?"

Haley turned slightly and pointed the barrel of the rifle at the ponderosa. "I set right there and listened to you two yap half the night." He turned back to Carr. "Didn't want to guide you two back in the dark, so I waited and enjoyed the conversation."

"Then you know." It was a flat statement from Carr.

"Yep, I know some. I know that you sure ain't no doctor, and I guess then that she," he nodded at the trembling girl, "ain't no nurse. Just what you had goin' with Whitman I don't know, but I suspect we'll all know soon enough."

"We haven't done any harm to anyone," Carr said forthrightly. "You could just let us go, and take the wagon and horse back."

"Marc, please . . ." the girl was standing at the young man's side, and in the faint morning light, Haley could see the terror that she felt, as well as hear the agony in her voice.

"Shut up, Ali," Carr snapped. "You could let us go," he repeated. "We haven't done anyone any harm."

"You want to argue that with Paul Burton?" Haley's voice was sharp. "You want to argue that with the Bonitises? They got two boys most likely down with the typhoid too." He saw Carr, at the mention of the children, close his eyes. "That's right," he pressed on, "both kids. But maybe you already knew that. How do you suppose their chances would be right now if they had had a real doc at their side, instead of a couple cheatin' quacks? Because you ain't no doctor, despite what most everybody back in Ludlum thinks. People depended on you. Seems to me, the way it turned out, that they trusted their lives to you. Now here you stand, tryin' to tell me that you done nothin' wrong, other than a little horse thievin'? I got to admit, it was a pretty good show. I never liked your pal Whitman, but I kinda liked both of you. Until now, leastways."

When Carr spoke, his voice was a whisper. "What are you going to do?"

Haley swung the rifle over his shoulder. "Well, I reckon my job will be tryin' to keep the town from tearin' you apart until we can get you to the circuit judge. After that, it ain't my problem. If we leave right now, maybe we'll be back before the whole town's up. You'll be safe for a while, though at this point I can't see why I shouldn't just let 'em have you."

Without another word, Carr turned and began to gather the camp together. Haley stood impassively, occasionally shifting his weight off the throbbing knee. He noticed the girl was quivering violently, trying with little success to hold back the deep choking sobs that shook her body.

When they were packed, Haley rode in the back of the wagon until they reached his own horse, where he got off and remounted, following the wagon as it jolted back toward Ludlum.

CHAPTER 11

That morning dawned bright and cool, and I overslept. I had left the El Grande with a bellyful of beer, and I did what I usually can't do when I worry—I slept and slept hard. The nine o'clock sun blasted through the windows into the two rooms I kept above the newspaper office, and I jarred awake, realizing that the town was already ahead of me for the day.

Dressing hurriedly, I plunged downstairs and headed directly toward Milt Haley's office. In my eagerness to learn the resolution to the problems of the night before, I even forgot about breakfast. I was surprised to find the door of the marshal's office locked, and even more surprised to have my ensuing knock answered. In all the years I had known Haley, he had never felt the need to lock himself in.

Haley was haggard. He held the door open for me, then closed it directly behind me, and locked it again. The curtains were drawn and the room smelled stuffy and close. "I was wonderin' on you," he said quietly. "I got your wagon back." He poured coffee from the pot that always sat on the back plate of the Emerson in the corner and handed me the cup. He sighed heavily, his mind obviously on something else other than the wagon.

"I'm gonna ask you a whole bunch of favors, Patrick." I started to say something, but he held up his hand. "Lemme explain the whole thing to you. Carr and his lady friend are back in the cell getting a little rest."

"Lady friend? You mean his sister? What were they doing?"

"He ain't got no sister. Alice there is his gal friend. They ain't married, so that's what they said to make folks take to 'em. Sounds pretty good, you gotta admit. Anyhow, he ain't no doctor, and she ain't no nurse." Seeing my eyebrows shoot up, Haley smiled thinly and sipped his coffee. "That ain't the half of it," he said. "You remember Whitman, the guy got himself shot? He was a partner to these two. From what I can gather, he'd come into a town and stay just long enough to get himself quite a list of people and their ailments—where they hurt, why they hurt, everything he could. Works really good with old ladies that always got an ache. Anyway, he'd get quite a list and hand it over to Carr there. Carr would come into town and stay a bit longer, and my gosh, wouldn't everybody think he was smart, knowin' just what was wrong with them and all, after just a short visit."

"You mean he'd have their names on the list before he ever saw them?" I couldn't believe what I was hearing.

"Sure, why not? Whitman was smart. Hell, they're all smart. There ain't near enough doctors around these parts. With a little common sense and bein' a good actor, who's goin' to call their bluff?"

"Mrs. Gardner," I said. "Seemed to me she sensed something."

"That's maybe one reason why they decided to up and leave so soon. She's no dunce, and even Carr got to know that. Anyway, the typhoid scared them off—that and Miz Burton dyin', and findin' out folks in town was sick too. Anyhow, they lit. And your wagon was handy."

I slowly rolled a smoke, trying to imagine some of the rage and anguish that would spread like wildfire when the town woke up to this new day. "It's hard to accept," I said.

"I liked the guy. Even though I was beginning to wonder who was right and who was wrong, I still trusted him. I thought he was a doctor. I really did."

"So did everyone else," Haley said dryly.

"Town'll crucify him, you know that."

Haley coughed and shook his head. "Not if we can work it right. That's why I need you. You and Miz Gardner are the only ones that need to know."

"What are you saying, Milt?" I sensed that Haley had done a lot of talking, while I had done a lot of sleeping.

"I mean that until we get us another doc, Carr and his lady friend are goin' to go on just like they have been."

I think at that moment there was an audible thunk as my jaw hit my chest. "Hell, Milt, you know what you're saying? You just got through finding out that the guy's a quack, and now, with us right smack in the middle of a typhoid outbreak, you want him to go on being what he isn't fit to be—even to think about being. That's crazy. I mean . . . no, you just can't do it." I realized that my voice had risen to nearly a shout, and I stopped abruptly. The door to the cells opened, and Carr stood there, tall and blond, but with heavy lines under his eyes. He looked at me as if he expected me to charge him, and he remained in the doorway for several seconds. Seeing Carr standing before me, I found myself for a fraction of a second thinking of him as a physician, but the thought fled as I remembered the consequences of the game he and his partner had been playing.

I heard Haley's voice, almost a whisper, say, "But who else have we got?"

I spun on Haley in a fury, but his face was calm. "What do you mean, who have we got?" I pointed at Carr. "If what you tell me is the truth, and everything falls together so I'm sure it is, just what the hell do you think we've got here? Some town savior? Damn it all, Milt, this man's nothing but a two-bit crook. He and his girl friend took us for a ride through the brambles. If he'd been a real doctor, he'd have known what was wrong with the Burtons. Maybe been able to save Jody. Right now, Mrs. Gardner is probably working herself to death trying to save some children and probably everyone else in this town. We haven't alerted the town before now because we were waiting on advice from this . . ." and I looked hard at Carr and for the first time noticed how worn the man was, and for the first time saw the trace of wetness under his eyes . . . "this whatever he is," I finished. Haley remained silent. I shook my head. "Maybe he don't deserve to be hung, but that's sure as hell what's going to happen when the town finds out. And"—I jerked a finger at Haley—"he sure isn't going to practice medicine in this town, or anywhere else, if I can help it." I paused when I saw a glint of humor in Haley's eyes. "This is anything but funny," I said heatedly.

"I know that, Patrick," Haley said. "But you get up on your high horse so seldom that it kind of took me by surprise. And I'm not so sure," he continued with his own vehemence, "that you ain't right. In fact I'm not so sure that I would be heartbroke if this one got strung up by his thumbs. I ain't sayin' that what he did was right. I ain't sayin' that he and his lady friend didn't help put this town in the pickle it's in right now. But what I am sayin' is that we've got us a problem to solve, and he might just be able to help us some."

"You should give us a chance." Carr's voice came from the doorway where he still stood, and it was quiet and strained.

"About like you gave us?" I said, turning toward him.

"Sit down, Patrick, and let me tell you somethin'," Haley interrupted. "Much as I maybe hate to say it, I still trust this guy some. Enough maybe, for what we have to do. If we got the typhoid problem in this town like I think we do, then we're goin' to need some people that knows something about nursin'." Haley saw my mouth starting to work again and he quickly held up a hand. "Hear me out. We're already a couple licks behind. I don't know nothin' about sick folks. Never said I did. I don't guess you do either. Fact is, Miz Gardner is about all we have, 'ceptin' these two here. Now I figure that they can help along those lines. They know somethin', or else they wouldn't be able to take the rest of us for a ride. I think they can be useful."

"You think that for a minute anyone in this town is going to let them be 'useful,' Milt? If you're sick to death, are you going to let some quack work on you? I think you're crazy. Your plan's crazy."

"Ain't nobody has to know what he is."

For a long moment I couldn't accept that Haley had just said what he had.

"You mean you've got this crazy plan cooked up to let him just continue on doctorin' and let the whole town stay in the dark?"

"I ain't sure about no plan," Haley replied, "but I do know that right now his help may be more important to us than stringin' him up."

"And when it's all over, he and the girl just ride off, nobody the wiser?"

Haley shook his head again. "Nope, can't do that. But it seems to me that if we was to ship him off to another court district, like say Laramie or someplace like that, he just might get a little fairer trial than he would here." He looked hard at Carr. "And if he was to cooperate with us in any way he could, then maybe a judge might consider that, too. I ain't just sure, after we stop and think a minute, that this young feller spending the next twenty years in jail is just all that fair. What he did was stupid and against any law, but he ain't put no gun against anybody's head."

"It seems to me that you're forgetting a very dead Jody Burton," I answered.

"Maybe so, but look at it this way. Doc Farraday knew he had troubles that were big. I think he knew that when he came to see you that day he got killed. I think maybe he needed your help to get this town together to fight the typhoid. Whatever he was after, it didn't do him no good. But how many doctors you count that came forward after Farraday died? Fort Bridger refused us. Whitman came along, and he sure didn't help Jody. But he didn't do no worse than no doc at all. Then Carr come along, and I got to admit that he didn't do no good either, but he didn't do nothin' worse than no doctor at all. We both know that whatever good was done was done by Miz Gardner, bless her soul, and she's still out there doin' it while we're in here jawin'. Law's been broke, but now we all know where we stand. I say let them help that knows enough, or wants enough, to help. I think him and the girl can help some."

"How do you plan to keep everybody in the town from knowing the truth? And how do you plan to keep them from stringing you up once they find out, once this is over?"

Haley shrugged. "That's why I wanted you with me, Patrick."

"Thanks a lot. I'd look good next to you on a rail out of town."

"I think folks'd understand," he said simply.

I laughed. "You do? You sure got more faith than I have. I still think you're crazy. But I tell you what. If you can convince Mrs. Gardner, because she's going to be the mainstay here, then I'll help any way I can. If you can't convince her, and you go on by yourself, then I won't help. That's the way it is. If she sees some merit in what you got to say, then maybe there's some truth in it all."

Haley visibly relaxed. "Then let me tell you what we done so far. You're a late riser, and you missed part of the fun. I talked to Miz Gardner early on this morning. You know what she said? 'I knew right from the start he didn't know one end of a patient from the other.' That's what she said. But I jawed with her for near an hour, and she allows as to how maybe Carr and the girl can help change sheets now and then. She says that people listen to him, and that might be helpful too."

"You're slick, aren't you?" I said, and Haley laughed. "So tell me how you expect folks not to find out?"

"We don't aim to tell 'em . . . just yet. Simple as that. Not too many know. Just us, Miz Gardner. That's all."

"Don't you suspect that a few folks are going to wonder about last night, with you riding after a stolen wagon? Like Will Cavenaugh, for instance? He heard us talking."

"You got a good mind. Make something up. You didn't know he took it, but it's all right with you. He had to see somebody real sick down the valley."

"Like who? Nobody lives down that way except the Peppers this side of thirty miles."

"Then he was going for a moonlit night ride with his girl?"

"A hayride with a girl people think is his sister? They'd really wonder."

Haley shook his head. "You're throwing up a logjam. Like I said, you'll think of something that holds. You're good at that."

I sighed. "And how's it going to look with them working out of a jail cell?"

The marshal's eyebrows went up. "He ain't in jail, is he? He's standin' there listening to you throwin' problems around. His gear is back in the office, his bag's up in the hotel room with no one the wiser. Once we get you straightened out, we're headin' over to the telegraph office to get us some advice from Bridger . . . that's the least those bastards can do for us . . . and then we're going to get to work and lick this thing."

Carr was still watching me closely, his tired eyes locked on mine.

"What do you have to say about all of this?" I asked. The young man shrugged and stood up straight, coming away from the doorjamb. His voice, when he spoke, was without the usual hint of arrogance we had become used to.

"I think I can do it," he said simply. "Alice and I are willing to help if what the marshal says about a fair shake later is true. Course—" and there was a faint flair of humor in his face, "—we don't just have a whole lot of choice, now do we?"

"And I'm not so sure you deserve any, either," I snapped.

Carr actually smiled. "No, I suppose, from your point of view, we don't. I won't argue that. But we will help. We can help. I know more than just a little, and Alice is really quite skilled as a nurse. And I think that in at least one respect, you're wrong. People will understand. I wouldn't worry about the wagon thing. It'll work out."

"I wish I had your confidence," I said, and turned to Haley, who was sitting on the corner of the desk smoking. "What exactly should I do now, aside from lying about the wagon if someone should ask?"

"Meetin'," Haley said, standing up. "We got to have us a meetin'. Much as I hate to say it, I don't reckon your paper comes out fast enough to do the job. You're goin' to have to hoof it. We got to get a fair body together today for a meetin', to tell 'em to stay away from the creek, tell 'em whatever else we can after we talk to the doc at Fort

Bridger. We sure as hell got us one hell of a late start. I just
hope not too late."

"When do you want to meet?"

"Well now, let's say noon. That gives you near three more
hours to get folks together. Get 'em to come to the El
Grande." Haley hesitated. "Naw, hell, that's too small, and
some of the women, if they come, why they'd feel uncomfortable. Might as well make it the church. You do that, and
in the meantime, this gentleman and I will find out what we
can from the doc down at Bridger, and maybe even there's
some books in Farraday's office that will tell us something."

With a few more assurances from Haley, I left his office to
take up my new role as vocal town crier, trying to get people to come to a meeting without spreading panic. We
wanted people to come—enough at one shot would help
spread the information throughout the valley by word of
mouth—but we didn't want any more surprises. We'd had
enough of those already. But as I stepped out into the street,
I didn't yet realize that the young man with the tired eyes
who I had left behind with Haley was still determined to
play his game using his own rules.

CHAPTER 12

The church was quiet and cool. We were kind of proud of that building, and it gleamed whitely in the sun from the many coats of whitewash that had been applied over the fresh lumber from the head of the valley. I got there at 11:30, and propped the door open. I could see a few people out on the street, talking among themselves and headed in the general direction of the church.

Jay Williams, the parson, strode up behind me from his little house just beyond the church. He was a solid man, and in another calling would have made a good blacksmith.

"Don't know what you're all up to, but just don't muck the place up," he said firmly.

I grinned. "Thanks for letting us in, parson." I saw Haley and Carr walking up the boardwalk past Woodstock's, and excused myself, leaving the parson to usher in the folks as they came. Carr was keeping his stride down, matching the marshal's limp, and I met them in front of the livery.

"We got us one hell of a telegraph tab," Haley said, "if we was ever called to pay it. Bridger thinks they got some cholera down there with the Indians that may spread, and they're still only with two docs, so he ain't about to ride up this way. He did give us some way to go, though."

"Who's going to do the talking?" I asked.

"I should," Carr said without hesitation, and both Haley and I were caught by surprise. "It only makes sense," Carr continued. "These folks don't know the difference yet, and it would look pretty odd for one of you two to do all the talking while the town doctor stands by like a wooden Indian. If I got to bring this thing off, I might as well start from the beginning."

"What you say does make sense," Haley said. "I don't see any way around it." He turned to me. "What'd you tell folks about the wagon? Anyone ask?"

"No, nobody did. I didn't see Will Cavenaugh. But I was ready. I figured to tell him that Carr here was ridin' down to Fort Bridger real quick to pick up some medicine that couldn't wait. Hell, beat the horse and it's only a day and a half each way."

"Hell, you don't have to make a fetchin' hero out of him," Haley scoffed.

"All I could think of," I answered.

"Let's get to the church," Haley said, and limped off.

Carr looked pretty good. Tired, but then that was bound to help, I thought. By a quarter after noon, the church was buzzing. Folks were curious, and a few kept pressing Haley and Carr. Both men fended them off, and watching the show, I could see that Carr was deep in his role, with much of the smooth confidence returned. Haley pulled out his big watch, and motioned to Carr. Both men went toward the front, and Haley rapped with his knuckles on the rough pine of the pulpit. It became quiet almost instantly, and I saw the last of the townspeople sit down. In the second or two of quiet, I saw Carr searching the faces, and then saw him stop. I followed the direction of his gaze and saw Alice Lindsay sitting in a back corner, beside Mrs. Gardner.

Haley cleared his throat. "Young man here has a few words that I think is important we all hear," he said, nodding at Carr. The lack of the word doctor in his introduction jarred me, but I doubt anyone else noticed—except perhaps the two women in the back.

Marc Carr unbuttoned his jacket and stood on the first step of the three leading up to the sanctuary, facing the people squarely. When he spoke, his voice was crisp and clear, but almost soft.

"Thank you all for coming. I know it was inconvenient for some of you to take time out from your work. But we have a problem facing us that I think you all need to be aware of." He paused and looked down. When he looked up, it seemed that his face was that of someone much younger, much less sure of himself. And when he spoke, his voice was a mere whisper.

"I have not been honest with you." He let the sentence hang in the air, and immediately the palms of my hands turned liquid. "I came into this town in the company of a young lady and tried to provide some kind of medical service to you." I looked frantically over at Haley, but saw no reaction there. Perhaps I was reading into Carr's words something more than what was there.

"I told you that the young lady was my sister. She is not. She is my fiancée. We had hoped to be married." There were a few whispers in Carr's audience, but they fell quiet when he continued. "I did that because I felt you would think ill of me for traveling in the company of a young, unmarried, and unattended woman. But if that were all, we wouldn't have asked you all here today. I need to ask for your continued trust at a time you may not be willing to give it." I looked over at Haley again, and he was standing straight now, glaring at Carr.

"Don't do it, Carr." Haley's harsh whisper was loud in the church, but Carr, with a calmness I found incredible, ignored him.

"I am not a physician." The sixty or so people in the assembly sat stone quiet, as if they had been individually poleaxed. Maybe everyone else was accustomed to the odd turns fate had handed to Ludlum, but I found myself feeling astonishment mixed with apprehension. I had, after all, asked that people come to this meeting, and I was, whether I liked it or not, associated with this incredible young man who held all our attention.

"I am not a physician," Carr repeated, "but I have spent time in medical training, and I am not just a quack." The way he said it made it sound almost as if he was a qualified practitioner. "I have helped some of you, and I have harmed none of you," he continued. For the first time, whispers forced Carr to pause. When it was quiet he continued, and I found myself wondering why these townspeople were still in their seats. I concluded uneasily that they didn't know the whole story. Maybe we'd be lucky and they never would. "I still want to help, and I can be of help. It would be presumptuous of me to claim that you need my help. By all rights you can put me in a cell and bury the key. But that would be no solution for the problem we face right now." He raised his hand for every last scrap of attention, and I marveled at his consummate self-control.

"It has come to our attention that one of the most feared of all epidemics is lifting its head in Ludlum." The room was instantly dead quiet. "When he died, Dr. John Farraday knew that Jody Burton was seriously ill. He knew it was typhoid." With that one magical word, the noise in the church swelled. All that Carr had said before seemed forgotten as ashen face turned to ashen face and the words of protest poured out.

"Please," Carr shouted. "Please. Hear me out. There are at least three cases of typhoid, probably more, in the village right now. Mrs. Gardner," and he nodded toward the back of the room, "has been up nearly all night tending. But she needs help. I found out about the typhoid and I ran. I admit that. It frightens me just as it does each one of you. I did not know what to do. I do not have the experience, and I tried to leave town. Your marshal"—and he nodded at Haley— "caught up with us in the mountains south of here. I convinced him, during the course of the night and the early morning, to let me repair some of the damage I may have done by being less than completely honest with you."

"That cagey bastard," I thought to myself. "He's even taken Haley off the hook. He'll win these people over and walk out of here a hero on top."

"I am making a public apology," Carr said, "which you have no cause to accept. But believe me when I say that I do want to make amends. I do want to help. We have been on the telegraph to the physician in Fort Bridger, and he has given Mrs. Gardner and myself detailed instructions. I know enough to follow them. I know enough to help. I am free, at this moment, to devote every waking hour to helping. I can do nothing in a cell. Out of a cell, I here give my public word that I will not run again. I ask only enough of your trust to be allowed to help."

He finished and stood quietly, and the sixty folks sat, also silent. Carr turned and looked at Haley, and it seemed that the sixty pairs of eyes did the same, as if seeking other advice than what was in their own minds.

The marshal stepped away from the wall, and his scarcely heard oath seemed oddly appropriate. He turned and faced his congregation.

"I don't know what to say, and this thing didn't go just like I planned, but I for one see something in what this young fella has said. Anybody got anything to holler about?"

The room remained silent for what seemed a lifetime, and

then I saw the bulk of Chester Newston, a valley rancher, rise from his seat.

"I got to admit I ain't never heard the like. But I got to say this. What this here young man has said about himself don't interest me near as much as what he's said about the typhoid. We got to get movin' on this. Hell, I once had a splinter near four inches long drove in my arm when a bronc tossed me through a fence. One of the boys carved it out, not no doctor. When you need help, you get it where you can. That's that, I'd say. This young fella's out and done something scarce few of the rest of us would do in admittin' the error of his ways. Hell, me, I would have just kept a-runnin', and hoped old Milt here never caught me. The fact he's standin' there and askin' to help got to tell us somethin'. Now for sure, he's got a world of questions to answer before we're satisfied, but I know what typhoid can do, and I know that every minute we stand here and jaw is going to cost us bad. Damn, this here is more of a speech than I've made in some spell. So if you two has been talkin' to Bridger, then I say let's hear it. I've trusted Milt before, and I still do. I don't know this young fella from Adam, but if Milt wants to stand by him, well, then, that's good enough for me." Newston sat down and Haley looked grateful. Carr's face was immobile.

"Anyone else?" Haley asked. There was a pause, and we heard Mrs. Gardner's voice from the back.

"Get on with it, Mr. Haley."

Despite the gravity of the moment, there were a scattering of chuckles, and Haley himself grinned thinly.

"If nobody has anything to say, then I take it we can get a move on. Carr here has the last telegram we got from the doc at Bridger, and he might read it so's we know where we stand."

Carr immediately pulled a lengthy telegram from his

pocket and took a step or two toward the people facing him. "I have read, and this telegram confirms, that typhoid need not be the feared killer it once was. True, it is dangerous, it can be deadly, but at least we have some direction for fighting it. Dr. Patterson at Fort Bridger says, and I'll read his exact words, 'find the source of the contagion and eliminate it.'" Carr looked up. "We know the source. It seems that the epidemic began upriver, at the Burton ranch. We hope that situation is now under control. Dr. Patterson further adds that the illness commonly spreads by two ways"—and Carr read again from the telegram in his hand—"'by water supply and by linen or clothing soiled by the patient.'" He paused for a moment, scanning the telegram, then looked at the sixty faces in front of him. "We know that about a week ago, the bedding of the Burtons, both husband and wife desperately ill, was washed in the creek by a well-meaning neighbor. That neighbor, miraculously, remained uninfected. But another man, living just downstream, contracted typhoid of the most virulent sort. He has since died, adding to the tragedy of losing Jody Burton as well. We did not know Mr. Garcia was ill, and he died unattended." A few voices ran through the assembly. "But we do know," Carr continued, and the voices stilled, "that at some time, he probably struggled up and rinsed his bedding and slop bucket in the water of Ghost Creek. He may have done that more than once, until he was too weak to move the few feet from his shack to the creek. It is clear, then, that the source of the typhoid was at the Burton ranch, and was introduced into the water of Ghost Creek. That creek flows, as you all well know, through this village. You also know, painfully, I'm sure, that several in this very town use the clear creek water for drinking, and certainly many of the youngsters use it for swimming, particularly the small pool just behind this church."

"Before this morning," Haley interjected, "we just weren't real sure about all this. We sure didn't want a panic. And I got to admit that we was waitin' some on medical advice." Somehow, the way Haley said it, it seemed sure that he was referring to Fort Bridger, not to his struggles with a desperate young man fleeing from an out-of-control game. "I just hope to God we ain't too late. As of now, that damn creek is off limits, and I mean there just ain't no damn exceptions to that. I got Bud Brown workin' as a deputy, and him and me sure as hell is going to arrest anyone we see anywhere near there. It's up to you to keep the young 'uns to home, but I guess I don't need to tell you all that."

"So what we got to do?" This was a voice from a few rows back, but the speaker didn't stand up.

"Carr here's got more on that paper," Haley said, nodding at the young man.

"First, you must report anyone ill, immediately, to us. We will be in constant contact with Fort Bridger. Dr. Patterson says that anyone, even with just what appears to be a mild influenza, will be treated. 'If it isn't true typhoid,' he writes, 'the patient can only benefit from the treatment.' Next, he writes that 'the rooms of patients must be kept absolutely clean and free from contagious bedding or clothing, and must be thoroughly aired, with as much sunlight allowed as possible.'" Carr continued without looking at the telegram, "All milk or water must be thoroughly boiled before drinking. And perhaps most important, Dr. Patterson insists that at the very first sign or hint of illness, the patient must be put to bed and kept there until the close of the illness. I think . . ." and Carr paused, "that we would be wasting time to follow through every detail of the treatment now. What we need from you is absolute vigilance. With your cooperation, I think that between the marshal, Mrs. Gardner, and whoever else can help, we can overcome this epidemic with a minimum loss of life." When Carr said that, there was an uneasy stirring, and he sensed it. "Typhoid is serious, and I have no doubt, as much as I would like to say otherwise, that the illness will take some with it. But perhaps we can beat it by working together."

Carr turned and sat down on the step, and he looked wrung out. Haley moved to the center of the room again, and called the meeting over after telling the townsfolk to report anything to his office, to be used as a headquarters. I watched the people file out and saw more than a few stop to exchange a few words with Mrs. Gardner. It was also evident that not many had words for the young lady standing near her, but maybe that would change. Some kind of control had been established at last, but none of us could have predicted how easily that control would be lost.

CHAPTER 13

The typhoid gave us little chance. It soon became evident that the disease had spread long before we were really alert to its presence. Flowing in the stream, the contagion prospered, its virulence seeming to grow as it flowed into Ludlum. Approximately two weeks after Dr. John Farraday had first visited the Burtons and probably made the first unheard diagnosis, the chain of outbreaks had begun in Ludlum. A week after that, several cases were blooming viciously.

Elderly and overweight Mrs. Sillitoe had it, and none of us could decide how she had come in contact with the bacteria—she hadn't been a likely candidate for swimming in the creek behind her house, and in the first days of her illness, she steadfastly denied drinking from the creek. I found out later that she had, however, accepted a colander full of late garden greens from a neighbor, and that neighbor had thoughtfully washed all the vegetables, including the lettuce that would not be cooked, in Ghost Creek. That's all it took.

As Mrs. Gardner nursed the elderly woman, it was evident that she was losing ground. Following directions from Patterson at Bridger, she kept a scrupulous record of temperature and treatment. We had held our meeting on a Saturday. On Sunday morning, Mrs. Sillitoe's temperature hit 104, and diminished only one degree by evening. Early Monday morning, she did not respond to any ministrations, and her pulse became thin and rapid. I remember seeing

Mrs. Gardner standing on the front porch of the home, taking a breath of fresh air, and when I caught her eye, she merely shook her head and turned back inside. Mrs. Sillitoe died late that afternoon, her aging and faltering heart refusing to fight the disease any longer. After the undertaker had come and gone, Alice Lindsay helped Mrs. Gardner clean out the sick room, and when they too left, the house stood empty and quiet.

That evening I stopped by Haley's office, and the news there was worse than I had anticipated.

"Seventeen," Haley barked as I stepped through the door. "We've got seventeen down, Patrick," and he ticked the names off. I recognized them all—more than half were children. There was no predicting who would be hit. While the Bonitis children were gravely ill, their mother remained untouched. The random attacks left no room for logic.

"How's Carr doing?" I asked.

Haley shrugged. "What can he do? I ain't sure he even knows what side of the street to walk on anymore. He ain't had no sleep since Saturday, and Miz Gardner neither. They can't keep it up, neither one. And look at this here."

He tossed another telegram at me, and I caught it and read quickly. "You understand any of this?" I asked.

"Hell no, and neither does Carr. Miz Gardner was some help, but not much. Who does Patterson think he's talkin' to, a bunch of goddamn chemists?"

I looked again at Patterson's message, but even the neat hand of the telegraph clerk had not made translation of the medical abbreviations any easier. As my brow remained furrowed, Haley laughed shortly.

"Leastways there's one thing we both understood," he said.

"What's that?"

"Seems one thing that helps when folks begin to get wore

out fighting is a good belt of whiskey every now and then. That's mostly what Carr was givin' out before, so it may have done a little good after all."

I looked at the paper again helplessly. "Even if we knew what these drugs were, where would we get 'em?"

"Unless old Farraday had a stock in his office that us blockheads would notice, your guess is as good as mine. We're on our own, I guess. We tried to tell Patterson more'n once that we weren't no doctors up here, but I guess maybe he's too busy with problems of his own to notice."

"Anything I can do now?"

"Hell yes," Haley said without hesitation. "Why don't you go on down past Woodstock's there and see if they need any more people with the laundry. Maybe you can scout out some more volunteers."

I had seen the smoke before and was heartened by the operation Mrs. Gardner had organized for tending to soiled linens and clothing. It had become evident early on that not enough extra bedding existed in Ludlum to burn everything when it became soiled, so the elderly woman had put together the next best arrangement. Using two moderate sized metal-strapped stock tanks from the livery, several people had set up a washing and sterilizing process that turned out clean bedding nearly as fast as it was needed. Washed out first with dousings in frequently emptied buckets, the rinsed linen was then washed in the first of the two stock tanks, a hot fire underneath keeping the wood charred and the water nearly boiling. Liberal charges of lye were added, and the water was changed frequently. From that caldron, the wash was rinsed in the second tank, with an even hotter fire underneath. This water was in fact boiling furiously, and when the linen was rinsed, it was poled out and hung on a long line to dry in the sun. After each wash and rinse batch, the tanks were carried between stout poles and emptied in the level field across the street and then refilled from Woodstock's well. After seeing the process, I suspected that most of the linen had never been so clean.

Working in the midst of the heat and vapors was Alice Lindsay, and she looked as pale as the linen she washed. I came up behind her and took her by the elbow. She turned and leaned her pole against the tank.

"You need more help here?" I asked. She looked around her at the four others helping, and nodded.

"Some of these folks have been here all day. We need to catch up before nightfall."

"And how long have you been here?" I asked quietly.

She blushed and looked away. "Have you seen Marc?"

"No, but the marshal says he's doing his best."

"He told me last night when I saw him that he thought Kelly Bonitis was going to die." She looked up at me. "Kelly's the youngest one. He's not yet a year old."

"I know that," I said gently. "I'm sure he'll be all right."

"Marc saw him when he first began to have the fever."

"How do you know that?"

"Mrs. Bonitis brought him to the office, because he seemed so fretful. Marc said he sent her home after telling her that that was just the way Kelly was."

I remained silent, and her words came after a struggle. "He thinks that that was the first sign of the typhoid, before the temperature had really gone up enough to notice."

"What could he have done, even then?"

Alice stared hopelessly into the boiling water, then back at me. "He feels that a doctor would have known, or at least done more than he did. Now that he knows what was probably wrong, he feels responsible for the baby's being so sick. He seems to care more about Kelly, somehow."

I felt awkward. "I wish there was something I could say

that would ease your mind," I said, "but I guess that's just the way it is."

"But you hold us to blame?"

"Some, I guess. But I've heard of worse ways to take folks' money. The way I see it now is that you two were playing a game where you didn't hold all the cards. You got caught by circumstances that no one could have predicted." I sighed. "Blaming people right now isn't going to help. I was convinced of that after the two of you were caught and brought back here. But you both are going to have to realize that folks have long memories. When this blows over, then I guess we'll know what people really think."

She stuck the pole in the tank and lifted out the corner of a sheet. "When this all blows over," she repeated my words.

"It will," I said. "Things always do. Then we'll see." I turned to go. "We'll send you some help so you and some of them"—I nodded at the others politely working at the far tank—"can get some rest."

Walking back toward Haley's office, I was surprised to see a plumpish figure sitting in the chair outside his door. It was Mrs. Gardner, and she didn't look pleased.

"You look tired," I said as diplomatically as possible.

"Of course I'm tired," she snapped.

"Why don't you go home for some sleep?"

"There's too much to do for that right now. There will be time enough for that later."

The marshal came through the door with a cup of coffee in his hand. He gave it to Mrs. Gardner, who, despite a harrumph deep in her throat, took it appreciatively. He winked at me.

"Told her that if she didn't sit down for at least ten minutes I'd chain her to the chair."

"We need you through all this, Mrs. Gardner. Milt's right. If you fall on your face, we'll be in a worse mess."

The elderly woman glared at me. "I'm not about to 'fall on my face,' as you so graciously put it. I'm one of more than a dozen people who are doing what they can." She put the cup down on the arm of the chair. "You know," she said, and her voice dropped the tone of false gruffness she had been using, "this is the first time I've really seen anything like this outbreak. Oh, I've seen typhoid, don't you mistake that, but never like this. It's come so fast. I mean, usually, it takes more than three or four weeks to run its course, but Bertha Sillitoe lived really no more than a week, it hit her so hard. And some of these children that are so sick." She broke off and shook her head. "There's so little we can do for them, except try to keep their fevers down and keep nourishment inside them. They bleed from the bowels, and we have no idea what to do. They're so weak that they aren't even frightened anymore."

"Are any improved?"

Mrs. Gardner laughed weakly. "I wish to God they were. Maybe Ruby Brown, a little." Ruby was the ten-year-old daughter of Bud Brown, Haley's sometimes deputy. "We tried some of that awful turpentine mix that the doctor in Fort Bridger suggested. That young man wasn't sure he had it mixed right, but it seems to help. The poor girl's tongue didn't look quite so awful after a dose."

Mrs. Gardner's mention of "that young man" indicated that she may have thawed some in her estimation of Carr.

"How do you think Carr's doing?" I asked.

Shrugging wearily, Mrs. Gardner was noncommittal. "He wants to help, and that's the important thing. And I've got to admit that he knows a sight more than most. But it took some fast talking to even get the Browns to let him in the house."

"Has that happened in other homes too?" I asked.

"I haven't spoken to him about it, but I get the impression that he's had some trouble. But you know, I think most folks are glad to have any help they can." She started and pulled her watch from her apron pocket. "Goodness," she said, and stood up. "Thank you for the coffee, Marshal," she said, and walked hurriedly off.

"Corker, ain't she?" Haley chuckled.

I had rounded up some help for the linen washers, had dinner, and spent some time in the shop before Carr's problems came to a head. The trouble began shortly after eight, with the streets dark and Frank Bonitis coming home from a four-week cattle drive up through Colorado to the railhead. He had stopped at the El Grande, a few convenient steps from the livery where he kept his horse, for a drink to wash the long day and the trail dust from his mouth, to refresh before he went home. It was there that he heard about the typhoid, his family, and worst of all, about a young man named Marc Carr.

CHAPTER 14

I was working late at the office of the *Herald* when the first violence started. I heard a metallic bang, like someone hitting a bucket with a stick, followed by a shout, followed by the loud, authoritative *whump* of a shotgun discharging. We hadn't had any fireworks like that in Ludlum for some months—Haley presided over a remarkably quiet town. Typhoid was what was on people's minds, not the kind of frontier violence that springs up from time to time in any small town.

The shotgun blast got my attention and got it in a hurry. I beat a line out the door of the shop, and I could hear the yelling clearly, coming from across and down the street. I'm not particularly quick on my feet—pushing a pencil for exercise does little for the gut—but I made it across the street in good order. Rounding the corner past Homer Woodstock's store, I saw an odd sight. On any day but this one it might have been amusing. Frank Bonitis was drunk, obviously, and in the darkness I could see his large strapping figure swaying dangerously. Dangerous, because in his hands was the double-barreled twelve-bore I had just heard. Then, two things happened swiftly.

Yelling obscenities at the top of his lungs, Bonitis leveled the shotgun and let fly at a large stock tank between Woodstock's store and his house. The tank was full of water, and the shot pattern whooshed a bucketful into the air and tore out a clanging chunk of wood and metal from the opposite side of the tank. I heard a screech, and saw Mrs. Bonitis on the house porch, her hands fluttering ineffectually. It was only then that I turned and saw the figure huddled behind the stout tank, crouching down on all fours, some poor soul trying for all his life to imitate a mountain gopher.

Bonitis lowered the gun, still howling incomprehensible oaths, and fumbled for a reload. His wife remained safely on the porch, wadding her apron. I stood a dozen paces behind Bonitis, watching, and the thought never occurred to me to do something heroic. But I needn't have concerned myself.

The slight, limping shadow of the Ludlum marshal slipped by me, came up behind Frank Bonitis and yanked the shotgun, now broken open, from the man's hands as if the drunken cowboy was a child. Bonitis stumbled back a pace, confused by this interruption of his night's work.

"What do you think . . ." he said, but Haley cut him off. The marshal snapped the empty shotgun shut and swapped ends, holding it up by the last foot of the still warm barrels.

"You want this here scatter-gun bent over your drunk skull, Frank?" Haley roared, and stepped closer, menacing with the gun-turned-club. "What the hell do you think you're about?"

Bonitis recognized Haley, and the belligerence seemed to tame him a little. He turned drunkenly back and pointed at the figure behind the tank. Jerking out a stiff index finger, he cried, "That there bastard's killed my kids."

"Frank, you don't make no goddamn sense," Haley said, and he peered at the tank. "Whoever you are, come out from behind there."

I saw the figure gradually pull up to his knees, then evidently seeing no one pointing a gun in his direction, Marc Carr slowly stood up.

"It's you," Haley said, and his voice was weary.

"He's the one," Bonitis yowled, still pointing, and he took

a shaky step forward. Haley raised the shotgun again, menacing.

"By God, you just take another goddamn step, and then
I'll crack you one," he snarled. He looked over at Carr.
"What's this all about?"

But Bonitis wasn't through with his side of the story yet.
"He's killed my kids. Goddamn no good quack." He gulped
for air and it seemed like he was going to go on, but Haley
interrupted.

"Just shut up, Frank. You're goin' to wake half the damn
town, if you ain't already. Carr, what's goin' on?"

The young man shook his head, but stayed on his side of
the heavy tank. "All I know is that I was in that house"—and
he pointed at the Bonitis home—"and this guy comes bust-
ing in half lit, cussin' and carrying on. He was after me,
whoever he is, and he grabbed a shotgun from over the door
and chased me out here. If I hadn't ducked behind this tank,
he'd have blown me in half."

"Goddamn right," Bonitis said loudly. Haley turned and
fixed him with an angry glare.

"Carr," the marshal said, "this here is Frank Bonitis. He's
father to those two young'uns in there. Been gone awhile,
ain't ya, Frank? Where you been?" His tone now was more
conversational.

"Grand Junction," Bonitis grumbled. "Been gone four
goddamn weeks."

"Four weeks, huh? Well, let me tell you somethin', mister.
You're goin' to be gone a whole sight more than four weeks
if you don't get some sense through your head in one big
hurry."

"He's killed my kids."

"Oh, Frank," Mrs. Bonitis wailed, but Haley waved her
off.

"He ain't killed nobody. What's the problem in there, Carr? How's the boys?"

Marc Carr shrugged. "They're sicker than I'd ever care to see again. The older one, he's holding his own, and I think will come out of it just fine. Kelly, though"—and he paused—"I think it's only fifty-fifty. The turpentine seems to have done some good, though. Seems to have eased some of the abdominal distress."

Bonitis drew himself up to his full height, nearly a head taller than Haley, and his face was incredulous. "Will ya listen to this squirt. Milt, he ain't nothin' but a two-bit quack, ain't even no doctor, and listen to him talk. Adominal distress," he mispronounced. "I tell ya, he ain't goin' to touch my kids. I want a goddamn real doctor. This here quack's killed my kids, and I'm goin' to bury him for it."

"What you need is to sober up some, Frank," Haley said firmly. "We ain't got no real doc, and Carr here, he ain't done no harm, and your kids ain't been killed. Fact is, they would be dead if it weren't for this young man and old Miz Gardner. Let's go on down to my office and jaw some." He took Bonitis gently by the arm and the big man hesitated. His wife took another step down from the porch.

"Please, Frank," and her voice was so high it was nearly a squeak. "Don't fight no more with the marshal. The boys will be all right." Haley tugged a bit, holding the shotgun under the crook of his arm.

"Come on, now, you're all through for the night. Don't make it no tougher than it is." The two walked past me in the darkness, and when they were gone, I walked out of the shadows and over to where Carr stood. The few people in the street had withdrawn, and we excused ourselves from the distraught woman, allowing her to return to her children inside.

"Kinda close," I said.

Carr ran a finger over the torn edge of the tank. "Yes," he said, "I don't know how that man found out, but we're going to have to keep him away until those two youngsters are better."

"He's their father, Marc," I said. "You can't expect him to sit across the street for the next two or three weeks."

"Maybe when he sobers up, Haley can talk some sense into him."

"Maybe. Can I buy you a drink?"

Carr shook his head. "No, I want to go up to Farraday's office for a while and do some reading. Maybe make more sense out of all this."

"How are the boys doing, really?"

"Like I said, one's okay, if we can keep him on the track. Kelly, though, is one sick little boy. His fever's been above a hundred and four for three days now, and I can't get it down. I've used alcohol baths, even some ice water. But I'm always afraid the shock of anything more severe will do just as much harm. I just don't know. If there were some drug . . . but he's not the only one. I've been visiting about a dozen who are burning up just the same. And they bleed so. God in heaven," Carr said hopelessly, "I've never known anything like it. Mrs. Gardner says it's normal for typhoid, but how can they take it for so many days? Patterson says that they ulcerate in the gut, and then they can bleed so much that with the fever and all they just run out of strength. I guess," and he laughed weakly, "that's why he prescribed the whiskey for anyone really sick who can't hold anything else down. Gives 'em strength. But I just don't know."

"Well, I reckon you're doing all you can," I said, trying to sound encouraging. "I saw Alice down where they're scrubbing the linen. I guess she's been at it straight for more than a day."

Carr looked off into the darkness. "Yes, I haven't seen her

since dawn." He sighed loudly. "I just hope to God all this comes to an end soon. I really do."

"It will," I answered, but I was afraid that there wasn't much hope in my voice.

Carr abruptly turned. "Maybe I'd better go back to the house and make sure everything's all right before I leave," and he turned and walked toward the Bonitis home. Over his shoulder he said, "If Haley needs me, or if anyone asks, I'll be in Farraday's office when I'm through here," and then the darkness closed over his figure as he climbed the steps to the front door of the Bonitis home.

Trudging back to my shop, I heard loud voices coming from Haley's office. From the sound, maybe Frank Bonitis had come alive again and was objecting to a few hours' cell-time. I didn't doubt for a moment Haley's ability to handle the big man, however. I'd never seen the marshal bested in either a verbal argument or a physical one, and I figured that with his fuse shortened by fatigue, he wouldn't tolerate much fuss.

I sat up late that night, and from my room above the newspaper, I could see the light in Farraday's office. And on occasion, I saw shadows pass across the light and knew Carr was there and working, trying to find some piece to the puzzle that might mean life to someone elsewhere in the village who would be tossing and bleeding on a bed, staring glassy-eyed at death.

I wasn't idle, either. Our efforts to locate another physician had brought us only the cryptic messages from the doctor at Fort Bridger—messages that half the time were incomprehensible to laymen. Villages and cities at every other compass point were of even less help. Laramie, so many miles distant, had not responded at all. There was no answer from Evanston to the west and a telegram from Ogden advised us that of the three physicians there, one was too old to travel, another was out of reach with an emergency of his own, and a third had simply refused to leave his own patients to attend to ours. We were alone.

An idea had popped into my head the day before, and I had been working steadily, or at least as steadily as conditions would permit. The story lay in front of me now, and I was pleased. If help wasn't available near at hand, then Ludlum must reach out wherever possible. I picked up the copy and read through the story once again, making sure I had missed nothing.

The headlines I had written were designed only to grab another editor's attention—I knew full well they would write their own if they used the story.

DREAD DISEASE STRIKES TOWN

Men, Women and Children
Struck Down by Typhoid

———   ———

Elderly Woman and Self-Styled
Quack Are Only Help for Residents

———   ———

Physicians Urgently Sought
During Hours of Dire Peril

———   ———

ENTIRE TOWN MAY VANISH
IF ABANDONED BY NATION

The multi-decked headlines were a little farfetched and certainly plenty sensational, but I felt justified. The story that followed was in the same inspired style, but there was little to lose.

Ludlum, Wyoming Territory, is fighting the Typhoid Fever. So many have been struck down, of every age and station, that local residents have nearly given up hope.

Not only has the dread disease spread through the normally pastoral valley, but residents are also without the ministrations of a physician of any kind.

At present, an elderly woman, Mrs. Lucy Gardner, is leading the fight against the disease. Experienced through many years of tending injured and ill ranch and mill hands, she is nonetheless at a loss to treat the Typhoid effectively—a task that would strain the resources of the most accomplished physician.

Her only help comes in the form of those village residents not yet ill, who volunteer their time and efforts at her direction. In addition, a young man who had earlier posed as a physician but was in truth nothing but an itinerant panhandler, has renounced the error of his ways and is staying on in Ludlum to help as ever he might, in company with his "nurse."

The village recently lost its only physician to a tragic accident, only days before the outbreak.

All efforts to secure medical help in the area have met with failure. Although the disease is now well entrenched in the village, town officials are seeking assistance from whatever source, of whatever distance.

Physicians who are disposed to travel to Ludlum will have their expenses paid from the village coffers, as well as receiving the eternal gratitude of all who will benefit from their coming.

Any who would answer this appeal are urged to begin the journey with haste. Confirmations of arrival may be wired directly to Ludlum, Wyoming Territory, in care of Town Marshal Milton Haley.

After a final reading, satisfied with the story, I gathered it up and went downstairs and out the front door. I was planning to telegraph the story directly to the appropriate desk of the Chicago *World Telegraph* to the east and the San Francisco *Evening Post* to the west, as well as the Denver *Tribune* to the southeast. My hopes lay to the east and southeast, since by train travel the trip might be made in as few as five days. San Francisco, with the mountain ranges between, was a distant hope.

I wanted to show the story to Haley before wiring, so that he would know my plans. I couldn't see that he would object. He didn't. Bonitis was apparently asleep out back, and I handed the story to Haley, who sat with his sore knee once more propped on the desk. He had been no more successful at sleeping than me. Reading slowly, word by word, his face was impassive until he finished.

"Couldn't have writ no better myself," he said, and grinned. "I didn't know we was about to vanish, but it'll make ears prick up, I suspect." He handed the copy back to me. "Glad we're going to pay their way. Probably be out of your hide."

"I figure we ought to try anything at this point," I replied. "Who knows. It might bring us some help. A week or two from now, we're apt to be just as bad off as we are now."

Haley nodded. "Send 'er off. Wake up old Smitty and have 'em earn his keep. Tell old fast fingers that the village's picking up the bill. He oughta be used to that by now. I'll cover any objections the old village fathers come up with, though I don't expect none."

Half an hour later, the story, complete with the lurid headlines, was singing across the wires to Chicago, Denver, and San Francisco. I couldn't help wondering about the reaction of the operators at the other ends, laboriously writing out the entire story, no abbreviations, no stops. At the end of the story, I had my name and position as publisher added so that the receiving editors wouldn't make a basket case on first glance. I thanked the finger-weary operator, and he grumpily assured me that, even if he was disturbed from his sleep once more, he would make sure I received any return messages as they arrived.

It was the middle of the night and my telegram would be lying on some editor's desk when the operator walked in early in the morning. As it turned out, the reply was prompt. I wasn't awake when Smitty pounded on my door. Hauling out of bed, I looked closely at my watch, and groaned at the hour. But excitement took over, and I strode to the door. When I saw Smitty, his eyes red and bleary, I immediately snapped awake.

"You got a message," he said, his voice noticeably triumphant.

I grabbed the telegram from his hands and read the scrawl of a half-awake operator. The message was brief and to the point:

Confirm Typhoid story earliest. John Tushfield, ed., World Telegraph.

Chicago had come through first, and I was elated. Dressing as quickly as I could, I half ran with Smitty back to the telegraph office and watched as he swiftly keyed out a response. Tushfield was obviously impressed with the story, but like any top-notch newsman, he was making sure he was not being hoodwinked—making sure the story had indeed come from Ludlum. The telegraph office must have been within a stone's throw of the *World Telegraph* building, because Tushfield's response to my confirmation was soon on the wires. Smitty tore it off and handed it to me, and I eagerly read what I wanted to hear. Tushfield was running the story, unchanged, except for a larger headline, in that day's edition, on page one. I was particularly gratified by the last line of his final message . . . "glad to help."

I slapped Smitty on the back and dug out a dollar, pressing it into his hand.

"Ain't necessary," he began, but I cut him off.

"Buy yourself a drink, Smitty. I want any other messages the minute they come in."

"You'll get 'em. Think the story will do any good?" I had never suspected that the story would fail to bring help, but Smitty's question caught me off guard.

"If it doesn't, it doesn't. But it seems like it's the last thing we got," I said. "I just hope to hell it works. Must be close to a million people read those papers all over the world. Now all someone's got to do is make it here soon enough to be of any help."

I walked rapidly back to Haley's office, but the building was closed, and I remembered the hour just as I was about to pound on the door. Everyone needed sleep, so I backed off. Still too excited, I looked down the street and saw the light still on in Farraday's office.

"Christ, he's still at work," I muttered, and walked to the steep steps that led up to the office. Light streamed out through a small crack in the door, and I knocked gently. There was no answer, and I pushed open the door and entered. Carr was at Farraday's desk, and several volumes were open in front of him, all but covering the smooth oak surface. His head was down on the desk, and he was fast asleep, his cheek resting on the open pages of Tilson's *Theory and Practice of Medicine*. A pen in his right hand had stopped its note-taking, and in the early dawn light, the oil lamp continued to burn patiently.

I left as quietly as I was able, and stood for a few moments on the step outside the office, looking out across the quiet village.

"I hope to God someone comes," I said to the quiet air, and started down the steps.

CHAPTER 15

The initial excitement of a possible response from outside the valley was soured later that morning . . . September 22, and the twenty-second day since John Farraday's death and the outbreak of the typhoid.

The weather was hopeful, the balmy air caressing, and the sky a bright, almost eye-hurting blue. But that was the extent of the good news.

Alice Lindsay had apparently taken her station at the laundry area early on, and she collapsed just before noon. Not from typhoid, several said, but simply from exhaustion. She had been up nearly all night with Marc Carr, poring through the textbooks that might offer some hint of assistance, then had apparently left the office shortly before my arrival there early in the morning—not to rest, but to stoke the fires for another day's grueling work. After her collapse, she was taken to the room in the hotel and put to bed, insensible.

Shortly afterward, Mrs. Gardner trudged by Haley's office with worse news. Two more had died during the night—fifteen-year-old Harold Adams and eighteen-year-old Millie Scott. Harold had been one of the town's renowned hell raisers. It was said that no privy was safely on its foundations when he prowled at night, despite the frequent whippings from his parents. Haley had caught him red-handed more than once, but the punishments that had been handed down seemed to make no dent on Harold. The typhoid put a stop to it all.

Millie Scott had been a dumpy, homely gal who worked patiently with her widowed father managing Scott's Mercantile, Homer Woodstock's only competition in Ludlum. She had gone quietly and quickly, Mrs. Gardner said.

"And," she sighed, "there are at least three new cases, all from the south end of town."

Haley banged his metal cup down on the table. "Damn it to hell, how's it spreadin'? Everythin's as clean as it can be, from what I can see. When's it goin' to let up?" He sounded almost plaintive, and I had never seen him so frustrated.

Mrs. Gardner wearily shook her head. "Hard to tell," she said. "It's hard to tell. From what I know, this may still be from the first contagion. It's not unusual for some diseases to wait two, maybe three, maybe four weeks before coming to the surface."

"Is there a single goddamn chance . . . pardon the language, but is there a goddamn chance that people's still so stupid as to get near that creek?"

"No," I answered, "people are avoiding it like the plague," and I laughed weakly at the pun.

Both Haley and Mrs. Gardner ignored my feeble attempt at humor.

"No, I think it's just the normal course of things," Mrs. Gardner said, and rose to leave. "I've told you what I came for, and I've work to do." She looked at me. "I do so hope that we have an answer from your story."

"No more than I," I answered, and held the door open for her. After she had gone, I turned to Haley, who had slumped down in his chair. "Along with all the other bad news, how's it going with Frank Bonitis?"

Haley gazed balefully at me. "I sent him home."

"Oh?" I was surprised the matter had been resolved so quickly.

"He seemed like maybe he'd cooled off some. At least, he promised no more rough stuff."

"Did he say he'd let Carr attend the two kids?"

"Nope. He said he didn't want to see 'em. I passed the word along to Miz Gardner, and she said she'd look in. That's all right with Bonitis, long as Carr doesn't show his face. Thing that worries me is if one of them kids dies. Frank's blamin' Carr, and swears to go after him if anything happens."

"Sounds like he'd be better off in jail, then," I said.

"Can't lock up the whole goddamn village. There's more'n Frank holds no good will toward Mr. Carr and his gal friend. All we can do is hope to keep 'em separate till everythin's over. Try and keep the lid on. And that might not be so goddamn easy. People's nervous, and they're going to be lookin' for someone to take it out on, soon enough."

"Maybe you ought to see Carr out of town, then."

"You talked to him lately?"

"Not today."

"Then don't bother even thinkin' that. He sees it as his debt to pay. Bet you five to ten that if I was to run 'em out of here, why he and his lady friend would be back before nightfall. I'd end up with 'em both in jail, is all."

"Wouldn't that be better than maybe some of the alternatives?"

Haley shrugged. "Maybe so. I'm just hopin', Patrick. That's all I'm doin'. Just hopin'. The way I see it, we need them both. Other folks besides me realizes that too. Other than Miz Gardner, he's all we got that knows anythin' at all about doctorin'. I can't see my way to send 'em off, when there's folks that benefit. I'm just hopin' I can keep the hotheads, mostly Frank Bonitis, settled down. Maybe I'm wrong. Maybe I'm flat wrong. And maybe I ain't, that's all. I can't do much with them that's sick, but maybe I can keep peace between folks. If I can just do that, then that's somethin'. But Christ, I'm tired. Everybody is. Tempers like two-inch dynamite fuses, Patrick. You do what you can, I'll do what I can, and we'll all pray like hell."

We were interrupted by a frantic knocking on the door, and I moved to one side and threw it open. Smitty stood there, his face bright with excitement. "You got a message," he said, and thrust a paper into my hands. I quickly unfolded it, reading quickly.

"Good or bad, Patrick?" Haley said laconically.

"Depends," I replied. "The editor in Chicago wants more information for another story in tomorrow's paper. 'Let's keep the pressure on,' he says." I looked up. "Must be a slow news day back there, to play this up for more than one day, with us a week's travel away. He wants the number dead so far."

"I guess we can provide that easy enough."

"I might as well take a minute and go back with Smitty and take care of our man. If nothing else, we'll go down well known."

I followed Smitty out into the sun, and we nearly ran into two breathless souls headed pell-mell toward Haley's office. In the lead was Zeppy O'Connell, the twelve-year-old daughter of Luke and Bea O'Connell, a prosperous couple who ran the government assay office near the north end of the village. With Zeppy was Bud Brown, whose daughter Ruby was holding her own against the typhoid. Ruby had kept Bud and his wife from being much help elsewhere in the village since she had taken sick, but they both took their turns down at the washing tanks, and Bud helped Milt whenever he could. Ruby and Zeppy were inseparable companions. Somehow fate had spared Zeppy the fever.

"Milt!" Bud roared, slipping past me and plunging into the office. "You gotta find someone to help. It's Mrs. Gardner." My stomach slammed tight when I heard that, and I saw Haley come to his feet with a start.

"What's wrong?" he said shortly, poised like a cat.

Brown gasped for breath from his run, then blurted, "I think it's her heart. She was workin' with Ruby, her and Zeppy about to change the linen and all, when all of a sudden she couldn't breathe or nothin'. Zeppy and me got her into a chair all right, but she can't breathe through all the pain she's havin'."

"Good lord," Haley spat, and came out of the building as fast as his gimpy knee would allow. As he passed me, he paused long enough to say, "Find Carr and get him the hell over to Brown's. If you can't find him, find someone who knows what to do. I'll be over there." And off he went, Brown on one side, Zeppy O'Connell on the other.

Forgetting the telegram, I started off, then stopped, trying to figure where Carr might be. As a starter, I huffed up the stairs of Farraday's office, but the door was locked. I turned and saw Smitty still standing in the middle of the street.

"Check around up the north end," I yelled down, "check every house. I'll go down to the south end and see if he's about down there." I ran down the steps, past Woodstock's, and saw that Carr was not down by the wash tanks. Inadvertently I found myself glancing at the Bonitis home, but I knew I didn't need to search for Carr there. After checking three more homes, I felt a surge of relief when I saw him walking, head down, up the middle of the street. He heard me puffing as I ran up to meet him, and his eyebrows shot up in surprise at my unaccustomed exertion. It took only a moment to explain the emergency, and before I had finished the second sentence, Carr had broken into a jog, a pace he

held until we had nearly reached the Brown home. When he
stopped, I nearly ran into him and was startled to see him
sag against the railing of the steps, head down, face pale.
After a few seconds, he seemed to recover. He looked sheep-
ishly at me as I stood out of breath and speechless with
effort, and he partially straightened up. "Too tired, I guess,"
he said. "Surprised Mrs. Gardner's held up this long."

With that, he seemed to quickly gain composure, and he
strode through the rude gate and up the stone steps to the
house. I released my hold on the gate post and followed
him.

Mrs. Gardner was sitting in the chair, all right. By the
look on her face, she wasn't about to move a fraction. Both
hands were clasped together at a point just under her throat.
She was pale and sweaty, with her eyes half closed. Carr
was instantly at her side, and I saw him taking her pulse,
gently, at the neck. She opened her eyes fully and looked
straight into his face.

"Is there a lot of pain?" he asked quietly.

Her voice was barely audible. "Feels like a train," she
said.

"Has it let up any?"

This time she merely nodded slightly.

Carr straightened up. "I don't know what to do, except I
think it's important that we get you lying down, so your
head is down, don't you think?" Again the slight nod. "Let's
take it real easy then." He motioned to Haley, Brown, and
myself. "There's four of us here, and we're going to pick you
up and just lay you down on the floor, on that thick rug.
Maybe Zeppy here will find us something to put under your
head." He motioned the girl, and she was off like a shot.
"Let's just get two on each side, and move her gently. Don't
make her do any of the work. None at all."

It was no problem with the four of us. In seconds, we had

Mrs. Gardner stretched out, albeit not too primly, on the floor. Zeppy produced a pillow and Brown handed Carr a blanket. Carr again was at the elderly woman's side, his voice low and confident—a confidence I think none of us, including him, felt.

"From what you say, it sounds like you must have had a little heart spell. You've been at it much too much."

"There's a need," I heard Mrs. Gardner say softly, her voice distant.

Carr patted her hand. "Yes, there is. There's a need for you to relax and rest, and let others help. Mrs. Brown will be here shortly, and she knows what to do. Have you ever had heart trouble before?"

Mrs. Gardner shook her head slowly.

"Then maybe it isn't serious. You know as much as I do, no doubt a whole lot more. But we both know that you have to rest. I don't know anything else to do. When you're feeling no more pain, then maybe we can safely move you to your own home and your own bed."

"This is ridiculous," Mrs. Gardner said, this time her voice a little stronger. "I'm feeling better already."

"You're the one person we can't take any chances with," Carr said firmly. "You have to rest. If you don't, you know what will happen." He looked hard at her until their gaze met and held. "You know that if you keep this up, especially right after an attack . . . you'll be dead by morning." The elderly woman said nothing. "You know that's true," Carr repeated. "You've got to help yourself, and the town . . . and me," he added softly, "by taking care of yourself. We've lost too many." The room was silent, all of us standing there, until the tension was broken by a moan from the bed.

For the first time since our arrival, we remembered Ruby Brown. Carr stood up and moved to the bedside. Ruby turned her head and looked up vaguely, but I don't think she really recognized the young man, or anyone else. Carr reached down and put a hand on the girl's forehead, then took her pulse. He looked at Brown. "Her heart is strong still, and she doesn't feel as hot as some. Tired out, though. Just like everyone else."

He turned and knelt by Mrs. Gardner again. "Do you think it would help if we gave Ruby a little more stimulant?"

"I was fixing to do just that," Mrs. Gardner whispered. "It's over on the sink."

Carr turned to Brown. "Where's your wife?"

Brown shifted nervously. "Down at the laundry. She said she'd be back before long."

"Well then, you do it. Your daughter is just worn out, that's the problem. Mrs. Gardner suggests that we give her a little stimulant, something to help her fight. She's in pretty good shape, and it will help." He took the brown whiskey bottle from the sink and handed it to Brown. "See if you can get her to take an ounce or so now, then again at mid-afternoon. If she doesn't have any problems, give her another ounce before you retire tonight. She may take it better mixed with milk."

"That's a powerful lot of booze," I heard Haley say from where he stood leaning against the doorjamb.

Carr turned quickly and snapped, "She's a powerful sick little girl, Marshal. She hasn't been able to eat sufficiently for several days. Whiskey has considerable value as a fast source of stimulation. Dr. Patterson says so. The book says so. And Mrs. Gardner says so. What we really need is for everyone to leave this room that isn't needed. Mrs. Gardner, if you are somewhat comfortable, I think you should remain where you are for a time, then we'll arrange some easy way to get you home. Mrs. Brown should be back soon enough."

While Carr bent down and exchanged a few more words

with the stricken woman, I joined Haley outside the room.
"He's really playing the part, isn't he?" I said.

Haley looked back through the door into the sick room, at
the little girl in the bed, at the elderly woman supine on the
floor, at the young man now earnestly talking with Brown.
"Only difference now is that he's playin' the part alone,"
Haley said.

CHAPTER 16

The second long telegram to the *World Telegraph* included everything I could dig up on Ludlum's outbreak—number struck down by the disease, number of children, number of adults. And, although I felt somewhat uncomfortable doing it, I led off with the news of Mrs. Gardner's collapse, saying that "the last barrier preventing the Typhoid's eventual victory has fallen."

I had not mentioned Carr's role again, preferring to wait and watch developments. He was doing an admirable job, but we didn't need a hero just yet. What we really needed was a doctor.

With Mrs. Gardner flat on her back and needing some tending herself, the load on everyone else increased. And so did the threat of pending violence.

On the afternoon of the twenty-third, Mrs. Bonitis tumbled into Haley's office, obviously upset. The words came out in a gush, but it wasn't difficult to piece together the story. Without Mrs. Gardner, no one seemed sure of what to do. Although the routine of treating the disease was as firmly established as was possible through the instructions of the physician at Fort Bridger, still the presence of a third party seemed to ease the burden. And with little Kelly on the verge of losing his fight, Mrs. Bonitis was frantic.

Her husband, however, was adamant. He would not tolerate even a glimpse of young Mr. Carr in his home, and it was Carr who had access to several medicines from Farraday's larder, and more important, some knowledge of their use. The young man's reading had discovered other possible options for treatment, including mild doses of antipyrine, a drug of some benefit in reducing fever. The textbook had also mentioned other drugs, but Carr was either unsure of the dosage preparation or of the interpretation of the labeled specimens on the shelves of the late physician's office. He had wired Patterson at Bridger, and Patterson had shot back immediately that larger doses of quinine were of value, but that the young man should not hesitate in experimenting within reasonable ranges with any of the preparations. Carr had had a difficult time determining what Patterson had meant by reasonable ranges, but the texts offered some help. Despite the dubious help, Carr had mentioned more than once that he felt he was following guesswork— but with several patients, guesswork was all the hope that was left.

One fact was sure. The benefits of brandy were obvious. Patients who feebly vomited any other food seemed to be able to cope with small amounts of liquor. The brandy, together with sanitation, sponge baths, and some experimentation with drugs had seemed to maintain the status quo of several victims, while their bodies fought the typhoid.

But there were others with such extreme cases that nothing seemed to work. Kelly Bonitis was one of those, and it was incredible that he held on to life at all, a small, wasted bundle taking up only a corner of his crib.

Mrs. Bonitis, knowing she was losing one of her own, wanted Carr at the bedside, for whatever good he could do. Frank Bonitis wanted Carr nowhere near his home.

"I don't see much I can do," Haley told the woman. "Your husband has every right to say who comes into his home."

"But the child is dying," the woman wailed.

"I'm sorry, ma'am. I truly am. But that don't change nothin', far as I can see. Now if Carr was a real doc, why then, it'd be different, maybe. But I can't force a man to let someone who ain't a doctor treat his kids."

"But can't you at least talk to him? See if you can reason with him?" Mrs. Bonitis had hold of Haley's sleeve.

"I can, and I have, ma'am. Last time they got together, your husband, he let fly with a twelve-gauge. Now I figure he's doin' well just lettin' Mr. Carr stay alive, with them in the same territory together. He blames the young fella for your kids gettin' sick."

With feet almost stamping with frustration and hands balled into fists at her side, Mrs. Bonitis cried, "But Marshal, it doesn't matter anymore whose fault anything was. Don't you see? All that matters is that they are sick and Dr. Carr is the only one who knows the medicines."

Haley looked long and hard at the woman, knowing that despite all that had happened, she still considered Marc Carr a physician. At a loss for anything else to say, he finally capitulated with a less than optimistic promise. "I'll try again, ma'am. But your husband's set, I know that." He held the office door open for her. "I'll talk to him tonight. I'll buy him a drink at the El Grande, if he'll come, and we'll talk it over. Do good to get him out of the house, anyway. But you know I can't promise you nothin'."

Late that afternoon, I got the telegram I guess everyone had been hoping for, me especially. It was from Chicago, but they weren't asking for another story. They were telling a town that had almost given up hope that maybe some salvation was on the way. The telegram, surprisingly lengthy for a business that is notorious for pinching pennies, informed us that, with the help of the *World Telegraph*, one Gilbert Parke, newly minted M.D., was on his way as fast as the Union Pacific could puff its way across the Midwest. Not a word had been heard from Denver or San Francisco, but that ceased to matter now.

In my jubilation, I still had time to wonder what the *Telegraph* had managed to say that had convinced a physician so rapidly. I suspected, and correctly so, that Parke would provide the answer, if and when he arrived.

I told Haley, and then spread the word around the town, hoping that the news would lift some flagging spirits. But promises of physicians had become old news. Most accepted the announcement without reaction, preferring not to have hopes dashed again.

At close to eight o'clock, Haley walked to Bonitis' and waited on the narrow front porch for Frank to come out. Bonitis grudgingly agreed to accompany Haley to the El Grande for a few moments, and Haley noticed how worn and haggard was his face. Neither man, as they walked through the heavy doors of the saloon, saw Mrs. Bonitis slip into the darkness from the back door of her home.

Chase brought both men a stein of beer, and Haley took his time, letting Bonitis talk. The cattleman was an independent sort, a top drover who could take his pick of drives, selling himself as a kind of free-lance foreman. He preferred working only sporadically, and Haley guessed that the man had money that didn't come from his trail-driving work. When he wasn't on the trail, Bonitis was a good family man, spending his time at home with his wife and two children. The obvious fact that he stood to lose one, maybe both, of his youngsters lay hard on his shoulders. Haley liked him, and understood how helpless the man must have felt.

"How's Mrs. Gardner?" Bonitis asked, bending low over his beer.

"She's had quite a spell, but I reckon she'll come out of it all right. From what she says, it's her first attack. She knows rest is the best cure, but goddamn, it's a pack a work keepin' her pegged down. She don't take kindly to others takin' her share of the load." Haley purposely avoided mention of Carr's name.

"You figure us to get another doctor from that yarn Bassett sent off?"

Haley shrugged. "Looks that way. We been stung before, but maybe this time's the charm." He paused. "No tellin' how long, though. Maybe a week, maybe a month . . . maybe never."

Bonitis fell silent, lost in his own thoughts. Finally he folded both hands behind the stein and looked across at Haley. "Kelly's slippin' away."

"I know that, Frank." He hesitated. "The other ladies been of any help?"

"Nobody can do nothin' with typhoid. Not now." Bonitis sighed heavily. "Maybe early on, somebody coulda done somethin', but not now. I ain't done it before, but I pray a lot now. That's all I can think to do."

Haley took the plunge. "You know, I ain't sure you been just all that fair with the young fella. He's done a lot of good . . ." and that's as far as the marshal got, for Bonitis interrupted him with an icy glare.

"That's bull, and you know it. Yeah, I ain't so stupid that I can't see that he's workin' his butt off, tryin' to make good. But I still can see that he don't know anythin'. And I still can see that if John Farraday'd been alive, Kelly woulda been taken care of from the very start."

"That don't mean that he can't do some good now. He knows the medicines better'n anybody else. Christ, Frank, with Miz Gardner down, he's the *only* one that knows even where to start, other than keepin' the sheets clean."

Bonitis waved at Chase, and another round of beer flowed. "Milt," Bonitis said heavily, "my mind's made up.

One of two things is going to happen. Either nature keeps Kelly alive, maybe until we get us another doctor, or he's goin' to die. But I sure ain't about to turn him over to some kid that took me for a ride in the first place. No siree."

"That's foolish, Frank."

"Maybe so. But that's the way it is. And I don't see as how you can force it, neither."

Haley shrugged and leaned back in his chair. "It ain't up to me to force nothin'," he said. "Long as you leave Carr be."

Bonitis looked up sharply at Haley. "I was drunk the other night. Sure, I'll let him be, and that's more than he deserves. I'll let him be just as long as he keeps out of my trail. I got more important people to fret about, one of 'em not yet a year old."

At that point, Homer Woodstock came in, and he headed over to the table. Homer and Frank Bonitis were pretty good friends, and Homer also tended to blab. He didn't hesitate now.

"Hey, Frank. I thought you said that young quack weren't going to get within a mile of your place," he said, and slid into a vacant chair. Bonitis put down his beer slowly and turned to Woodstock.

"He ain't."

"The hell he ain't," Woodstock shot back, and Haley's hand gripped the stein tightly.

"What you talkin' about, Homer," the marshal asked.

"I mean I seen him go right up the front steps of Frank's place just as cool as anything."

"When's that?" Bonitis' voice was deadly.

"Hell, just a couple minutes ago. I was checkin' down at the tubs to make sure the fires was out for the night. Saw him go by and right up to your house. Yer missus was with 'im."

Bonitis turned and glared at Haley. He didn't say anything, but Haley could read the message in his eyes.

"Stay put, Frank. Let it ride," Haley said, but Bonitis was already on his feet.

"You bastard. You pull me on over here so's that he can slip in behind my back?" He started to move quickly toward the door, and Haley knew his only chance was to delay the man long enough for Carr to get out of reach. He knew the worn-out young man was no match for the hardened drover, especially when Bonitis was sober. The initial advantage was Haley's, since he was between Bonitis and the door, but his game knee made his movement awkward as he tried to shift sideways to block the aisle. And he underestimated the blind fury that drove Bonitis. With rattlesnake speed, Bonitis grabbed the back of the cane chair in which he had been sitting and swung it in a vicious arc. Haley saw the chair coming and twisted, throwing up his arm. But that twisting motion was more than his knee would tolerate, and it buckled under him with an agonizing wrench that threw him off balance. The chair crashed down on his upper arm, and he spun to the floor. Bonitis was past him and out the door before he could roll and make a grab for the man's ankles.

"Jeez," Woodstock said, and the silence in the saloon was monumental. Chase came around the end of the bar and grabbed Haley under his arms, helping him to his feet.

Haley grimaced, taking the weight off his leg, simultaneously holding his left arm. "Chase, gimme your scattergun."

"He's gonna hurt someone," Chase said, his voice calm.

"No kiddin'," Haley snapped. "Now gimme your goddamn bar gun."

"You ain't in no shape," Chase said, but moved to the bar and took the sawed-off double from a shelf below the till. "You need help?"

"No, you stay inside. All of you," he said, sweeping his gaze around the saloon at the half dozen frozen occupants.

He swung on Woodstock, and hefted the scatter-gun. "Except you. You can help me on over there. Maybe we won't be too goddamn late." Woodstock started to say something, then thought better of it. Holding the gun by the stock, Haley used it as a short cane, the twin muzzles digging into the wooden floor.

"That thing's loaded, Milt," Chase called, now anxious, but Haley ignored him. Woodstock followed uncertainly behind, not much help at all.

CHAPTER 17

Marc Carr had Kelly Bonitis' tiny head cradled in his left hand, and was carefully spooning tiny amounts of milk laced with brandy into the infant's mouth. He was sure that the child's temperature had abated somewhat, but he wasn't sure that pulse was any stronger. It was still painfully obvious that the infant's bowels were hemorrhaging, and Carr knew that the child needed any sustenance that would be kept down.

"We're not going to let you go," he said softly, and spooned another portion of the sweet milk into the infant's mouth.

"It's a good sign that his temperature's down in the evening," he told Mrs. Bonitis, who stood behind him watching carefully. "If he takes the food tonight and again in the morning, let's try another small dose of the antipyrine and see if the temperature's really beaten. He's still bleeding, but I think the turpentine is too strong. So does Dr. Patterson. Even Mrs. Gardner agrees it's best to let nature do the healing. Did his temperature break this morning?"

Mrs. Bonitis shook her head. "No, in fact it seemed so high. That's why I had to find you. Before, he seemed better in the mornings."

Carr tried to make sense of the information, but all he could remember was a paragraph in the textbook about false remissions before another stronger onslaught of the fever.

High morning temperature was one characteristic. But maybe . . .

He watched Kelly feebly swallow some of the milk, and then, as he was taking another spoonful from the cup, heard the heavy, running footsteps on the porch. Without hesitation, even though Mrs. Bonitis had said nothing about her husband, Carr knew what the footfalls meant, knew as the door burst open behind him.

He turned his head far enough to see Frank Bonitis standing in the doorway, but he did not take his hand from the infant. "Your son may be . . ." he began to say, but Bonitis moved across the room with frightening speed, brushing his wife out of the way with one hand. Carr had just enough time to carefully lay the infant's head back down in the cradle before Bonitis' hands closed around his right arm, sending the spoon flying.

Carr was young and athletic, but the days of endless work had taken their toll. Bonitis snapped him across the room as if he were a floppy pillow, and he slammed into the door frame with such force that the air crashed from his lungs in a loud whoop. He heard the woman cry out, and dimly saw Bonitis' two fists, locked together, coming at him like a sledge. He tried to turn, but the fists were faster, the brutal blow hitting him in the short ribs and sending him out into the parlor of the house to land on his hands and knees. The vicious, silent attack was not over, and he knew it. But all power to move had left him, and he remained on the floor, his forehead resting between his hands, his breath replaced by a sharp, piercing agony. He hardly felt the kick that sent him sprawling, then he was bodily picked up and dragged to the door of the house. Motion became a blur, with a brief image of someone else off to one side coming up the porch steps. Then he was kicked forward, to twist and buckle over the low railing, falling backward. The edge of the porch flooring beneath the rail slammed into the small of his back, and then he was face down in the drying grass, senseless.

Haley had tried to formulate several plans as he lurched awkwardly down the street toward the house. Woodstock followed silently behind, then stopped at the corner of his store, letting Haley continue on alone.

The marshal was still wondering how to handle the drover when he began to mount the steps of the house and saw Carr hurled out the door, to slam into and flip backward over the railing. On the second step, and somewhat to one side, Haley was well below Bonitis. Having disposed of the immediate threat to his child, Bonitis turned and saw Haley coming up the steps, and saw the shotgun. A man used to fighting with his hands, he took almost a negligent swipe at the twin barrels that Haley held as a threat.

"This ain't your fight," he hissed.

"It ain't no fight, it's murder, Frank. You'll kill that boy, if he ain't dead already, and by God I won't let that happen."

"You won't let? You think I'm simple? You think I don't know why you got me over to the saloon just now? Sure, so this punk could sneak in behind my back. I always thought better of you than that, but now I guess I was wrong."

"You've done enough," Haley snapped, and backed down a step so that his weight rested on his good leg, lifting the shotgun up again.

Bonitis spoke and moved at the same time, fast and deadly. "I'll figure when I done enough," he snapped. "I aim to teach him that I mean what I say."

Haley miscalculated, assuming that Bonitis would move toward Carr, but instead the man feinted and lunged directly at the marshal. As a result, it was easy for Bonitis to smash the barrels of the scatter-gun aside, step in and slash at Haley. The blow caught the marshal full across the face,

snapping his head back. He lost his balance, frantically
scrambling to catch the post at the bottom of the steps, but
missed. He fell heavily, the shotgun beneath him. Untan-
gling his legs, he turned painfully over on his back, and in
the dim light he saw Bonitis on the other side of the porch
near Carr. Twisting in panic, Haley pulled the twelve-bore
out from underneath himself as he saw Bonitis draw back
his foot. Haley cried out, and Bonitis ignored him. Seeing
the kick begin its downward arc, Haley lowered the barrels
and jerked the forward trigger.

The flash and smoke of the shotgun obscured everything
for a long moment, until the night air gently lifted the pall
of smoke up and over the house roof.

Haley struggled to his feet, holding his left knee stiffly,
and hobbled over to Bonitis. Both of the drover's hands
were holding his right leg high up on the thigh. Haley saw
the blood pumping rapidly through the man's fingers, then
Mrs. Bonitis was between the two men, on her knees beside
her husband.

"Frank, I told ya. You got to let him be," Haley said, his
words hopeless. He realized he still held Chase's shotgun,
and he tossed it up on the porch. Mrs. Bonitis was trying to
staunch the flow of blood, with no success, and Frank Bonitis was grimly silent, his lips pressed tightly together, his
face pale. The woman, sobbing, tried to speak as she
worked.

"Frank, Dr. Carr said that maybe Kelly would be all
right. It's still too early"—she choked, the tears running unchecked down her face—"too early to tell for sure. Frank,
you've got to let him help."

Haley knelt down and looked closely at the leg wound.
The charge of horseshoe nails Chase kept in the gun were
designed to leave no second chance, and Haley knew it
would take more than a tourniquet to stop the bleeding. But

knowing no other way, he began to tear a strip from the ragged pant leg. Bonitis' voice stopped him. From between clenched teeth, his eyes still closed, the drover rasped, "Let me the hell alone. You get off my property."

"Frank, sit still. You'll bleed to death if you don't get some sense, and get it quick," Haley said, and continued his efforts. Bonitis mumbled something else, then quite distinctly, Haley heard his last words.

"It ain't fair," Bonitis said, then sagged over onto his side, face in the weeds. Mrs. Bonitis cradled his head, and Haley frantically tried to find the lacerated artery, but after another minute, it ceased to matter. The blood stopped all by itself.

Stiff from his fall, Haley stood up, looking down at the woman, rocking back and forth with her husband's head in her lap. "I'm sorry, ma'am," he said, the words empty. He turned and saw Woodstock standing by the corner of the building, forms of other spectators behind him.

"Get some help," he yelled, and stumbled to Carr, who lay motionless where he had fallen by the porch. "Where do we go from here," Haley whispered to himself as he bent down.

They buried Frank Bonitis the next morning. All in all, I guess that Mrs. Bonitis bore up pretty well, at first, anyway. She seemed to concentrate every fiber of her being on the infant. Her other child had never really been terribly ill, and as that child slowly recuperated with each passing hour, the infant slipped a little. Carr's earlier intuition had been correct—the temperature was not broken, but had been only a diversion while the illness worked up its final charge.

Seeing the child slipping from her, Mrs. Bonitis did everything she could, including nearly killing Mrs. Gardner. Pale and weak, the elderly woman nonetheless crawled out of bed and dragged herself to the infant's cribside. But Kelly Bonitis died while she was there, just about dinnertime. Tired as she was, sick as she was, and bone weary as she was of seeing her friends and neighbors buried, Mrs. Gardner still had a good round of tears to share with the distraught woman. Then one of the neighbors helped her back to her own home, where she lay down on her flowered quilt, hoping that her pounding heart wouldn't explode. After a few moments, the pounding subsided, and the elderly woman slipped into a deep sleep.

Marc Carr was carried to his room in the El Grande lying flat on an old door that someone had found. I went and fetched Alice Lindsay, who was working again up the street. She had heard the gunshot but had paid no attention. Now she ran to the hotel, her hands in tight fists. She reached the room just as they were transferring Carr to the bed, and she watched anxiously as he was carefully stretched out.

Haley told her briefly what had happened. "I'm afraid he's bad hurt," he said, "but it's all inside. You'll know what to do as well as anybody else. I wish to hell now that old lady Gardner could make it up here, but she sure as hell can't."

He helped the girl remove Carr's coat and shirt, and the ugly bruises around his lower ribs were already coloring deeply.

"You've got to find a doctor," Alice said suddenly and forcefully.

"One's on his way."

"From?"

Haley looked over at me, and then back at the girl. "Chicago."

She seemed to sag against the bed. "With bruises like

that, and so pale, I know he's bleeding inside. He's got to have medical help."

"Alice," Haley said, his voice soft and patient, "that's a problem a lot of folks are facing right about now."

And despite what any of us might have wanted, we were all helpless. During that long night, Alice Lindsay stayed in the room with the unconscious Carr, and for a couple hours, I kept a morose Milt Haley company in his office. But even that didn't offer any solution, and well past midnight, I finally stumbled off to a few hours of troubled sleep.

The next day, despite our weariness, and despite the sadness of seeing Frank Bonitis buried, it became apparent that the iron grip the typhoid held over the town was weakening some. I didn't see Haley for much of the day—I guessed that he was making the rounds in the village, limping from one house to another. He had given his grudging consent to allow Mrs. Gardner's presence with Kelly, but had said that there was little I could do. Late in the afternoon, shortly before receiving word that the infant had died, I even tried taking a turn at the washing tanks, but there was less to do even there. After dropping one sheet in the dirt, I resigned that post and went back to the newspaper office.

I became involved in editing another piece of stolen copy and looked up only when I felt someone's presence in the room. Milt Haley stood in the open doorway leaning against the jamb, his face pensive. I returned his gaze without offering a word. After a long silence, he said, "Kelly up and died."

I sat back and laid the pencil down. "I guess we aren't surprised."

"Nope, I guess we ain't," Haley answered quietly. "I'm going to look in on Carr. Want to come?"

"How's he been doing?"

The marshal shook his head, then shrugged. "Girl's been with him all night and all day. Still out, I reckon. Don't know if he's ever goin' to come around. Hell of a deal."

I stood up. "Let's go, then."

It seemed that nothing had changed in the room of the El Grande. Carr lay as still as death, eyes closed, hands at his sides. The girl closed the door behind us, and I couldn't believe she was on her feet, so long had she forced herself to remain awake and watchful. Haley told her as gently as he could about Kelly Bonitis, but it was evident her concern at the moment was entirely with the beaten figure on the bed.

"Have you heard any more about a doctor?" she asked, and her words came with the quickness of near hysteria.

Haley shook his head. "I'm sorry."

Her eyes pleaded. "Mrs. Gardner?" she asked, and her voice broke.

The marshal gazed at the girl, their eyes locked. "I won't ask it of her," he said. "She don't have the strength. It'd plumb·kill her, what with her getting up and tending Kelly to the last hour. I'll be honest with you. I ain't even told her, and I don't suspect I will, 'cause I know what she'd try and do. But I ain't sure there's anythin' she could do that you ain't already done." The silence hung heavy in the room, and then Alice nodded once, quickly, as she resigned herself.

"We'll just have to wait, then," she said, her voice tight.

At that moment, the three of us seemed to realize simultaneously that Carr was watching us. He lay still, eyes bright, and a sheen of sweat on his forehead.

Alice went to him immediately, and bent over, kissing him lightly on the lips.

"I'm bleeding inside," I heard him whisper.

"Just lie still. There's a doctor coming," Alice said, and took his hand.

"Doctor?" His lips formed the word, but it was inaudible.

"Yes. They got word. From Chicago."

A faint smile lighted Carr's face, then vanished. "How's Kelly?"

Alice looked up, first at Haley, then at me. Her eyes pleaded, but neither of us knew what to say. Carr saw the exchange, and knew. He closed his eyes, and his head turned slightly away.

"Everyone tried," Alice said. "They really did. Even Mrs. Gardner came over, but there was nothing they could do. The fever hadn't really broken."

Carr turned back and looked at her, his hand coming up off the bed a few inches to rest on her forearm. "How are you?" his lips formed.

Alice held his hand tightly. "I'm fine, tired, but fine. And now you're going to keep me from my work." Carr smiled again, the expression just a ghost. His eyes moved and locked on Haley's.

"Any more people sick?" his lips said. Haley shook his head.

"Couple folks even a little better. The other Bonitis boy is going to be just fine. I hear even old Paul Burton's restless to be on his feet."

The young man nodded and looked back at Alice. "We got it beat," he said, and this time his voice was clearly audible. He was about to say something else when a spasm passed through his body, and his eyes first registered a look of surprise, then blank pain, then closed tightly. He lay rigid for a moment, then seemed to relax. After another moment, his eyes opened, and fastened on Alice. She was crying openly now, holding his left hand in both of hers.

"Stop that," he said, again quite clearly. Slowly he reached up his right hand and held her by the shoulder as she bent near the bed. He moved his head, looked at Haley and me, and then at the door.

"We'll be outside," Haley said, and nodded at Carr. His eyes held Carr's for a moment, and then Haley turned and limped from the room. I followed.

"Let's go downstairs," Haley said. "I think I'm going to get drunk and stay drunk all night."

We did go downstairs, but neither of us drank. Instead, the marshal stood by the window looking out across the dark street.

"Was that the truth?" I asked.

"About what?"

"About no new cases of the typhoid."

"Hell yes, it was the truth. We had it licked, and now this." He took a seat on the last step of the stair landing, stretching his left knee out in front of him with a grimace.

Before long, I heard quiet steps behind us and turned to see Alice coming slowly down the stairs. It was obvious by the look on her face that it was over. She stopped two steps from the bottom and waited for Haley to pull himself to his feet, then stepped down on the last step, her eyes on the same level as the marshal's.

"Do you know what he asked?" she said, her voice small and distant.

Haley shook his head, and she looked over at me. "Is there really another doctor coming?"

I nodded. "He's on his way now. From Chicago."

"He asked me to stay here and work for the new doctor, if he'd have me." She stood straight, but the tears were coming back now, running unchecked down her cheeks, dripping unnoticed onto the front of her dress.

Haley looked down at his feet, then at Alice. "That's about the best thing I can think of," he said. "Right now, we got to find a place for you to stay a bit. I'll take care of things here, and I think it would make a whole lot of sense if Patrick here'd take you on over to Miz Gardner's place. She's got the room there, and she needs somebody right about now, too."

CHAPTER 18

On the day before Christmas, Billy Pepper missed the wood block and laid his foot open with an ax, right through the boot. Ben Pepper rode his boy into town, holding him while the blood leaked through the bandage and dripped down the flanks of the puffing horse. I saw them ride by as I sat behind my desk, contemplating a New Year's front page.

In his own calm way, Dr. Gilbert Parke received the youngster, and as his nurse passed him the tools of the trade, he stitched the boy's injury as neatly as a spinster stitches the hem of a quilt.

"Dress that for me, will you, Alice?" he asked, rising to rinse off his hands. Alice Lindsay bandaged the youngster's foot quickly and faultlessly as Parke watched from across the room. In moments, father and son were gone, and Alice was cleaning up.

Parke watched her as he finished drying his hands.

"You still going to leave us?" he asked, neatly folding the towel and hanging it on the small rack.

"Yes."

"I want you to know that you've done just a fine job . . . from the very first. If there's any way I can be of assistance, don't be bashful."

Alice smiled as she put the instruments on the counter. "No, I'm just going home for a while, that's all."

"I won't ask if you're coming back. I can't say as I blame you for leaving. You know," Parke said, hitching up his trousers, "an editor friend of mine at the Chicago *World Tele-graph* bet me I didn't dare come out here all by myself to save what he called a dying town. He even paid my way, so he could tell his readers that his newspaper had a heart. He got his story, and I got here just at the tail end, but soon enough to know that you folks did one hell of a job. And I think that what you did, by way of staying on, was commendable. You should stay in nursing. You're a natural at it. I wish there was some way of influencing you to stay on here, or at least making sure that you'll be back."

"Thank you, Dr. Parke," Alice said, smoothing her dress. "But I've got to go home to New England for a while and think things out. I may well decide to be a nurse, but I've got to find out in my own time. I've been living for the past few months in a way that was not of my own choosing. I'm not complaining, and I'm not ungrateful. You've been wonderful to me, and the town . . . well, they've been more forgiving than I've a right to expect. But I have to take time out now and have a chance to think it all out, to find my own way."

"I guess it'll take a long time to get over losing that young man," Parke said.

Alice was silent, her fingers intertwined and quiet. Parke watched her face and recognized the emotion that still lay so close to the surface. He stepped over and laid a paternal hand on her arm. "Take comfort, during the rest of your life, and I hope it's a long and fruitful one, that you two paid your debts fearlessly and completely, and far more bravely than most of the rest of us would ever be capable of." She would not raise her face, and Parke felt a twinge of lingering sadness, the same feeling he had experienced when he first came to Ludlum, when the story of the young couple had first been passed along to him. Still new to the medical profession himself, he had had a difficult time imagining what thoughts had gone through the minds of the couple as they tried to work their way out of the situation they had helped to create.

It was late in the afternoon, and Parke was weary. After a few moments, Alice had finished her work, and as the conversation lapsed into a mutually accepted silence, she put on her heavy cloak and left for the day. The office was quiet and Parke thoughtful, standing by the window and watching the girl's fading figure pad through the darkness toward the old woman's home. Before many more days had passed, she would be gone from the valley, and Parke would look for another assistant.

As she vanished from view, Parke sighed and turned from the window to sit down at the oak desk that had belonged to another doctor in another time. He shuffled papers for a moment, then sat quietly, idly running his fingers along the binding of the thick Tilson text that lay at his elbow. A slip of paper preserved a spot near the front of the book, and even though he knew his favorite passage by heart, Parke opened the text and removed the slip of paper that partially hid the page.

He knew that no matter how many times in the ensuing years he read the passage, its meaning would always be tied as one with his memories of the girl and what she had been through.

As he recited the short paragraph, his lips carefully formed each word.

With purity and holiness will I pass my life and practice my art. Into whatever houses I enter, I will go into them for the benefit of the sick, and will abstain from every voluntary act of mischief and corruption . . . while I continue to keep this Oath inviolate, may it be granted to me to enjoy life and the practice of my art, respected by all men at all times.

But should I trespass and violate this Oath, may the reverse be my lot.

He closed the book, gazing at the ornate cover thoughtfully. Then he straightened up and pulled the blind over the window. Tomorrow would bring more patients, and he would need the rest.